John McKenzie is an ex-b⟨...⟩
He is the author of *City W⟨...⟩*
written seve⟨...⟩

GW00836677

are you boys cyclists?

john mckenzie

Library of Congress Catalog Card Number: 96–69697

A complete catalogue record for this book can
be obtained from the British Library on request

The right of John McKenzie to be identified as the
author of this work has been asserted by him in accordance
with the Copyright, Designs and Patents Act 1988

First published in 1997 by Serpent's Tail,
4 Blackstock Mews, London N4, and
180 Varick Street, 10th floor, New York, NY 10014

Set in 10.5pt Jansen by Intype London Ltd
Printed in Great Britain by Cox & Wyman Ltd.,
Reading, Berkshire

are you boys cyclists?

chapter one

∿∿∿∿∿∿∿∿

We went into the local sports centre and stood staring at the menu.

'How's about the wrestlin'? Ah quite fancy learnin' how tae wrestle,' said Jerry.

'Look, there's boxin' there,' I said. I could feel a slight jag of excitement. I knew what boxing gyms looked like, since I'd seen them on the telly and in films. We could skip and biff bags.

'There's rock climbin'. How's about that?' said Jerry. Suddenly, he didn't look quite straight. He was pulling at one of his curls, imagining shimmying up some precipice, no doubt, with the huge expanse of blue sky at his back.

'Fuck that, man. Ye can fall on yir heid at that game. It's dangerous,' I said.

I was dying to go to the boxing. I was amazed that there was boxing on offer. My big brothers had boxed. When I was hardly a youth, a man with a bent nose had given me free chips once after noting the family resemblance. Uncles I didn't know had boxed in booths in Australia. It seemed that practically everybody in the Lanarkshire town I came from had boxed at one time. I just wanted to have a look at it, to see what it was like. I was dying to go to the boxing.

'Dangerous?' Jerry was giggling, not caring about what

anyone else might think. People in track bottoms with fat sports bags walked past. They didn't give a shit about us either. 'Dangerous? Gettin' punched in the heid isn't dangerous?'

'We're no goiny git punched in the heid, Jerry. Ah'll keep ma glasses on. Hey, they might let us hit some bags.'

'Come on, man,' said Jerry. 'They dae karate here. Let's check that out.'

It seemed a lot more sensible. Instead of risking getting punched in the head, you could learn to kill with a single blow, turn your hands and feet into lethal weapons. But it seemed ridiculous to go to the boxing. I still looked like a hippy, after all.

'Ah'm scared tae go the karate, man,' I said. 'Imagine gettin' pissed, losin' your temper, an' punchin' your fist through someone's heid. You could end up walkin' about wi' somebody's heid encirclin' your forearm, draggin' the whole carcass along.'

We couldn't get into the karate. It was full. They let us into the boxing, though. I couldn't find my way out of a one-way street, so Jerry had to negotiate the labyrinthine passageways. Lockers and keys, and feeling awkward, but it's hard to go to places you don't know. You don't want to feel too nervous and you don't want to make a bad impression. Being a wee bit stoned doesn't help.

There's a long corridor with big rooms off it where you can see people through the open doors practising things like fencing and judo, or balancing on beams, or climbing ropes.

This isn't really the beginning. Most books have long, boring passages at the beginning which are supposed to establish character, setting, etc. You don't usually jump in with a guy called Jerry and a guy called Matt heading for some brain damage without explaining who they are, or setting the scene, or building up the ambience and that. Maybe I'd better establish some kind of beginning before I get on to the sex and violence.

⸺⸺⸺⸺⸺

I was reduced to carrying my suitcase and plastic bags around the streets when I landed in on Mora's flat. I'd stayed there for a couple of months before moving into the flat I'd just got evicted from. I really wanted to tell Jerry and Mora and Poisonous what a fuck-up the whole thing was, what with getting stabbed in the back by the three young women and having nowhere else to go. Jerry told me I'd had a phone call offering me the usual wee Edinburgh flat. I kept telling him how shitty everything was and he kept saying it was okay, it was okay. I had a flat. The man phoned up. Meet him outside the Meadowbank Stadium. It was a Saturday afternoon. He was a Meadowbank Thistle supporter. Jerry dressed me up. He had a black velvet jacket and a nice pair of trousers and shoes. They all fitted me better than him because, although we had the same build, he stooped a little. Off-the-peg clothes don't have the stoop built in.

⸺⸺⸺⸺⸺

The wee man had a moustache and very shiny shoes. He had an overcoat on. He must have been someone's batman at some time. Meadowbank had won, lost, or drawn. I can't remember which, but I was sure it didn't really matter to a Meadowbank supporter. I talked to him as we walked round a couple of corners to the flat he owned. Was there good parking in the area? I asked because my wife, who unfortunately wasn't in Edinburgh that weekend, had a motor car. I really talked up the wife. Young professional woman of substance with motor car. A schoolteacher or something like that. I'd advertised myself as a young married couple, just in case getting another place with the three young women didn't work out. He showed me the flat.

All the landlord has to do is ring the bell, and when the man answers, he says he wants to show the flat to someone. The man has to let him in because he doesn't own the flat. The dwarf does. He shows me round. I end up standing looking at two embarrassed people, the man and his partner, as the landlord talks away. Because we're standing in this couple's living room, it is embarrassing, but the people will be out on Tuesday morning. And I would return on Tuesday evening. The man gave me a key and one for my wife. We shook on it.

Have you ever imagined shoving someone by the throat up against a wall and then punching their face in till the eyes are like rotten tomatoes, and the teeth are all pointing at funny angles through the lips, or tinkling to the ground, and the whole thing really looks like raw pizza? If you do occasionally drift off into little reveries like that, you're probably a man. This is partly what this book's going to be about, in case you are wondering. Violence and sex. Movement between fantasy and reality. Written, as you may have noticed, without too many subordinate clauses and pointless adjectives, in an easy-to-read style. Also, without colons or semi-colons because nobody knows how to read them or write them any more. Neither will there be words like sugugulent, so that you can read this stuff without having a dictionary sitting on your lap. Actually,

I just made that word up, in case you were thinking of looking it up, but I promise not to do anything like that again. Suppose I'd better get back to the stuff you always get in the build-up.

~~~~~~~~~~~~~~~~

Suddenly, there wasn't an awful lot of anyone around. There was just me and a lonesome awareness of what I was doing, the way you know you'll remember all this somehow. This is moving into a new flat to live on your own, by yourself, for the first time ever.

No one ever believes it when I tell them about the mouse. It appeared on the first night. It was a Tuesday. The black-and-white TV had come in the taxi, but there was nothing on and I'd put it off and sat down at the table, which I'd dragged into the middle of the living-room floor. It was around midnight and I was going to start writing.

I hate it when writers write books about writers. I promised myself I'd never do it, but then again I'm not a writer, not a real writer, not a successful writer with a penthouse suite and lots of foreign holidays. As far as writing goes, I'm best described as struggling. In fact, I'm part librarian and part housewife. But I might as well write another book, since there's nothing else to do at this time of night, i.e., after the early evening news. I've no money or I'd go on an expensive foreign holiday instead.

I had the table in the middle of the floor because it felt right there. So you've got the typewriter on the table in the middle of the floor and the wee light's shining on the five-hundred-thousand-word pile of crap which I will, during the course of the next several months, reduce to a two-hundred-thousand-word pile of crap. This was my first novel. I spent six years out of the next twenty writing it and re-writing it and still nobody wants to publish it. This is because it's a pile of crap.

Just as I was about to start, I spotted the mouse. It was gambolling across the floor. Rolling over and jumping about and playing by itself. I sat there looking at it and wondering if there ever was a stupider mouse. Then I thought it must never have seen a human being before, but that struck me as unlikely since I'd just moved into a second-floor flat. Maybe it had gone mad. A rabid mouse. I got hold of one of the wee cardboard boxes I'd packed my stuff in and sneaked up on it. I couldn't believe it. I'd caught a mouse by putting a cardboard box over the top of it. What was I going to do with it? I didn't want a mouse for company, but I didn't want to kill it. I wasn't sure how to, anyway. Strangled mouse? So I left it under the box and went back to typing.

This is how to write a book that will never be published no matter how many years you spend on it. First of all, write all about yourself and what you were like as a young man, and about how all those bastards were rotten to you, especially women and university lecturers. Intersperse it with all that stuff about sex and drugs, and when you've got the half a million words take out all the funny bits.

Actually, if you were a woman this book might be a lot more interesting. Women writing dirty books make money. I'd like to pretend to be a woman and write a dirty book for pots of money, but I'm going to write this one first. There will be lots of sex in it. Don't worry. This book isn't going to miss being part of the wank industry if I can help it. Maybe I could change my name to Alison Main and then the dirty bits would be a lot more interesting.

The next night the wee mouse appeared again. When I'd finished typing the night before, I'd looked in the box and the wee thing had somehow disappeared itself. But there it was gambolling around again. It seemed to be taking little jumps in the air and then falling on to its back, rolling over and starting again. There was no reason for what it was doing that I could see, unless it was planning to set up classes in mouse aerobics.

I caught it no bother in a box again, but this time carried it through to the shower.

I should explain at this point that it was the usual small Edinburgh flat. There was a living room and a bedroom, with a small kitchen off the living room and a small bog and shower room off the lobby. I'd moved there from one of the usual big Edinburgh flats in South Clerk Street, with the huge kitchen, three large bedrooms, a big sitting room, etc. I'd also left three big women in that flat. Or rather, after the eviction, we all went our separate ways. Or they left me stranded and fucked off by themselves. Whichever way you looked at it, I'd moved from a big place with lots of people milling around into a small place with just a wee mouse.

I did not want to live with the mouse, so I took it in behind the shower curtain where the surface was obviously going to be slippery and frightening for a mouse once it escaped from the box. Then I went back to the huge pile of crap in the living room.

I was half expecting it the next night, but at the same time I could hardly believe it when it appeared again. And I put the box over it again and put it into the shower again.

'Get tae fuck out of this flat, mouse! Tell all your friends there's a fuckin' lunatic livin' here now! Awright?!' I shouted down at the mouse before putting the box on the floor of the shower space, and walking back to the living room. Then, two minutes later, I went back into the shower without switching on the light and put my head inside the box and delivered much the same message.

The next day there was no mouse in the box and that night no mouse appeared. I never saw another mouse in that flat before I got evicted again.

Nothing happens at the start of most novels. Pages in and all you've got is a guy and a mouse. Well, so far we've got the guy who's moved into this flat on his own. And he doesn't like killing mice. So although later on he's going to brain-damage and brutalise folk, we should keep in mind that he is a good person. But so far he could be anyone. I could make him a private detective who wants to write novels on the side. A murderer. Anything. I'm certainly not going to write one of those horrible books in which unemployed people make unsuccessful attempts to defeat, overcome, accept, or ignore the horribleness of it all. Certainly not. A wee bit of unemployment never did anybody any harm, not unless you've got bills to pay and children to look after, or whatever, and no money. I didn't have any more money than anyone else who was single and unemployed then, but I was unemployed because I wanted to be.

I might have wanted to be unemployed, but I did not want to be evicted. Everyone thinks it has to be your own fault when you get evicted. People don't immediately think the landlord must have been some kind of overcharging, exploitative bastard who should be publicly castrated in front of the Rent Tribunal. Not many people think like that anyway. But maybe I'm wrong. Maybe with landlords being able to lord it over you a bit more these days a lot more people think like that.

A dead giveaway mentioning the Rent Tribunal there. Of course, things like that have been disappearing ever since the fascist regime got elected in 1979. So this story is going to be set before 1979, in fact around 1977, the year I didn't go to work at all. 1977 isn't all that different from now except that everything is worse now. They had Rent Tribunals then. You could take your landlord to the Rent Tribunal once he'd decided to sell your flat from under your feet. And if he tried to evict you, you could fight the case in the courts and to get anywhere he had to prove greater need than you. You were secure in your rented flat then till the cows came home unless your lawyer failed to show up at the court on time and you lost by default. Bastards!

Living on your own is all right as soon as you get used to the idea that no one is going to visit you. If you wonder whether people are going to visit you all the time, you're anxious. You're fucked. You just need some time to settle into being on your own. But it was good to have the TV, even though it was black-and-white. I used to wait for the weatherman at night to read the Atlantic chart. In those days he had to walk from the Great Britain map into the Atlantic map, so that you got just the voice-over as he made the transition. The weatherman always looked dead nervous as he walked back into view.

A couple of months after getting rid of the mouse, that used to crack me up. I used to wait for that at night when I discovered it was on the other side from the man who talked to all the old people, and the lonely people, and the people who live alone. Please remember to turn off your TV set. No wonder people start hearing voices and think the electric cables are out to get them. It's all right to live on your own once you get used to the idea that no one is going to visit you, but a lot of crazy people live on their own as well.

I think I could call this the end of the beginning of the beginning. You know there are three people in one flat, called Jerry, Mora and Poisonous. You know there's another guy who doesn't even have a mouse for company any more, and three big women he used to live with have been mentioned, although not named. You also know that the person writing the book is a writer. I didn't really have to tell you that, did I? Just a bit of reassurance on my part. But I've decided to change my tactics. No more spending hours sculpting paragraphs of beauty. Nobody cared anyway. This book will be full of sex and violence. To hell with paragraphs.

When I was writing the first book about being a young man and everybody being rotten to me, I had a wonderful routine. I'd get up in time for 'The World at One' and start working at two. I'd finish working at six and read and watch the TV till it went off around midnight. Then I'd work till four in the morning. You can put half a million words through a typewriter and end up with only two hundred thousand if you follow a routine like that five or six times a week for months and months. Then I decided not to show it to anyone because it was still crap. I was in a gap, trying to think of what to do next, when Jerry arrived with his suitcase one night. Mora had thrown him out. It was partly because he wasn't getting on too well with Mora that Jerry had ended up going to the boxing. I was still wading my way through the half-million words of crap at the time.

⟨⟨⟨⟨⟨⟨⟩⟩⟩⟩⟩⟩

It didn't look like the boxing gym I was expecting. Some boxing gyms are really just huts. Some of them don't even have sinks to rinse the blood off your gumshield, but the Meadowbank Boxing Club is part of the Meadowbank Stadium so it was hard to know what to expect. Noise. Little explosions of sound as gloves thud into bags, or bodies, or off pads. Heat. There were big windows looking out on to the track, misted and running with condensation. The walls were wet. The whole place seemed to be sweating and the air was heavy with that beautiful, humid smell of hot, clean bodies at close quarters. The floor was red and the walls were white. Six or so bags hung from hooks in the ceiling. A little room bulged off at the side, big enough to hang two bags in. Apart from that there was just the ring, which was at ground level and almost set into the corner. And despite all the noise and all the sweat, all you could really see when you went into that gym was the ring.

I'd seen people sparring in boxing rings on the TV, but it didn't look anything like what these boys were doing. They were more like wild animals. There was nothing at all sedate about what they were doing. More like a cat-fight, whirling in a flurry of perpetual motion from one end of the ring to the next. Then back again. They weren't wearing headguards and they didn't stop hitting each other.

'No fuckin' way,' said Jerry.

'Fuckin' mental, man,' I said. 'Let's speak tae someone an' see if they'll let us dae some trainin'.'

'Aye, boys. Whit can Ah dae fur ye?' said the wee man.

It was hard to tell what age he was. One side of his face looked like it might have been hit by a shovel at some point, and then hit again at the other side to try to even it out. But it hadn't really worked. The point of his nose wasn't really a point any more and was pointing in the wrong direction anyway. He kept blowing air down one nostril for some reason. He said it was okay for us to do some training if we wanted to.

Jerry found a rope. A boxing gym is not the place to learn to skip. There wasn't anyone skipping at the time, but what Jerry was trying to do wasn't really skipping either. A vulture could have skipped better. It looked as if a vulture was learning to skip. We sidled over towards the wee room where we might draw less attention to ourselves. There were heavy bags hanging in there. We found a pair of mitts. I stood behind the bag and held it while Jerry tried to hit it. This does not look too elegant either. Another man came over to speak to us.

'Are you boys cyclists?' he said.

chapter two

~~~~~~~~~~~~~~~~~~~~~~~~

'Are you boys cyclists?' he said.

I looked at Jerry and waited.

'Naw,' said Jerry. 'Ah don't even have a bike.'

The man explained that it was my hat that made him
think we might be cyclists. I was wearing a peaked cap
with a hairnet attached to the back. I'd worked in the
steelworks for a year after leaving university and they'd
given me this hat as a safety precaution.

~~~~~~~~~~~~~~~~~~~~~~~~

You'd probably have to have worked in a steelworks to
see the funny side of that. If you're looking for such an
opportunity these days, you've had it, of course, since all
the Scottish steelworks are in South Africa or Korea or
somewhere. I started writing a novel partly set in a Scottish steelworks soon after Jerry came to stay in the wee
flat. But that was still in the future then. I was still wading
through the university novel when my doorbell rang one
night.

~~~~~~~~~~~~~~~~~~~~~~~~

Jerry arrived with a suitcase and a couple of plastic bags

and a green foam-filled sofa bed. I have no idea how he got the latter in a taxi. He'd said things were getting critical and I'd said he could always come and stay with me, but I wasn't really expecting him.

'The bed's brilliant,' I said, seeing it laid out there in a corner of the living room. 'You'll have tae fold it up every day because Ah'm never sure whit day the landlord's goiny show up. The landlord's the only problem Ah can see, but it'll be cool because you'll be at work when he comes round.'

Jerry was a lorry driver. This is a totally misleading piece of information. It's like saying I was a housewife. Maybe I was practising for later on, but I wasn't all that much good at being a housewife then. I used to let my dirty clothes soak day after day in the sink until the water went green. The dishes piled up on the draining board beside that until there were no clean dishes left. One of the women I thought I'd fallen out with when the South Clerk Street scene came apart, surprisingly wanted to stay in touch. She asked if I'd play with her at squash. She came in and slowly paced the living-room floor and then looked in the kitchen.

'Do you have rats, Matt?' she inquired.

She didn't believe the story about the mouse and it's a pity she's not going to play a bigger part in this book. I had to swop her over with my girlfriend, who will have to be in Australia during the entire course of this story for reasons that will become obvious when I get to the dirty bits. Girlfriends of writers don't like it when they write about sex. They think people begin to look at them funny after they've read it. If you wonder what I do during the weekends in this book, I drink home brew and visit people. I haven't really got a girlfriend, though I'd quite like to have one. But the one I had went to Australia for the entire duration of this story, the bastard, and has given me huge problems in sequencing and plotting.

The woman who isn't in the story any more always had a couple of eunuch boyfriends. Men used to ask her out on the assumption that they were getting closer to her sexual organs, but the Ice Woman didn't see it like that. Once she brought home a thin seventeen-year-old, but we all knew she spent all night tormenting him. She started getting visits first thing in the morning from this PE teacher, who seemed very old, at least in his forties. He seemed to be coming and banging her before going to his work. She was at teacher's training at the time. After that, she got a summer job being a gardener in Princes Street Gardens. She joined the Scottish Labour Party at its birth and paid a pound for me. Then she was unemployed. She didn't know what to do. I told her to apply to the Conservative Party and ask to be a secretary because she had the English middle-class voice. She got the job. She wanted to get off with Nicholas Fairbairn. A pervert kept coming in and asking for pictures of Maggie Thatcher. Now she works as an editor on the diaries of an eminent old socialist. This is the woman whose first boyfriend was an enforcer for the Richardsons, the big London firm of gangsters. She was at the Old Bailey watching him going down, twisting her pigtails. Obviously, she would be the most interesting person in this book if I kept her in it, but she isn't the one I got to tie up so I'm editing her out of my life.

The windows were always closed and the gas cooker was always on, even if just at a peep. I needed the kitchen constantly warm to maintain the supply of home-brewed beer. When Jerry came to stay, he put a pair of cowboy boots in the shallow cupboard set into the living-room wall. They rotted with the condensation. But unlike the big Edinburgh flats, it was warm. We walked around in teeshirts most of the time.

I knew there would be some changes with Jerry coming to stay, but he needed a place to stay and there wasn't really any choice in the matter. We went to the boxing together. He was my pal, I suppose. He'd been in the place two nights before he decided he'd have to go back to Mora's for some stuff.

'Is it goiny be awright?' I said.

He assured me it was. He was just going to pick up some stuff. Everything was going to be okay. She'd kicked him out and she would want all his gear out of the place. It was amicable, he said. It was going to be okay.

I was standing still at the edge of the couch, which backed on to the part of the room where the sink and the window were. Poisonous was sitting on the couch, saying nothing, his foot waggling at the end of a crossed leg. It looked as if someone had polished him up then placed him there, rigid and radiating through the silence.

Mora and Jerry seemed to be in perpetual motion, walking around, stopping, arguing, sitting, moving around. Even when they weren't in the room, me and Poisonous didn't say anything to each other. The atmosphere was very tense for us.

Mora looked like a twenty-three-year-old witch. She had on loose skirts and kept pulling a shawl close to her as if she wanted to fold in on herself somehow. And her back seemed hunched, her long curly brown hair straggling and unkempt. She looked down a lot and didn't seem to catch anyone's eye as she muttered to herself. When she wasn't muttering, she'd accuse Jerry of something. Her voice wasn't loud then, but whingeing. We never said hullo to each other. Was it going to be all right? Was it fuck! Then they were both sitting down in separate chairs facing the couch where Poisonous sat.

'You owe me one hundred and twenty pounds,' she said.

'Whit?' said Jerry, aghast.

Mora started hitting him with figures for this and that, and the next thing, and the next thing, and as well as that. It went on. She wasn't looking at him then either, but half spitting towards the floor between them while bending over, beating her fist against her thigh. The telephone rang in their old bedroom. Mora stood up and stamped her foot in annoyance, shaking her hair from side to side. It looked childish, petulant. She hurried out the room.

'It's for you,' she said to Jerry when she got back.

'Who is it?' he asked, surprised.

'Your mother,' she said bitterly.

No one said anything while Jerry was out of the room. Mora was clenching her teeth, and nodding, and rocking a little in the chair, rehearsing stuff. Jerry came back into the room looking almost at ease with himself.

'Whit were we talkin' about again?' he said to no one in particular.

'You owe me one hundred and twenty pounds!' she insisted, almost with a hiss.

'Okay,' he said. Jerry took his chequebook out then and signed a cheque. While she was scrutinising it, he smiled tightly over at me. 'Ready to go then?'

'Sure,' I said.

Mora said 'Well' and rubbed her nose as she stood up

to see us off, still looking at the floor. She seemed disturbed. Not angry, not irritated or annoyed. Disturbed. Embittered. Unhappy. There was nothing I could say to make it any better, since I'd taken sides by being there with Jerry. We ended up outside in the Meadows waiting for a taxi to come along.

'Was that awright?' I inquired, a little archly.

'Better than Ah expected,' he said, nervously laughing. 'My mother says she's sending me a cheque for five hundred quid.'

They'd been the most obviously wonderfully happy couple. They were always smiling and laughing and hugging each other at one time. Everybody said it. A perfect couple. She'd thought he was going to solve all her problems. She didn't really have any problems, but he was supposed to superman them out of the way somehow. That's what she was looking for, the knight in shining armour. It all started going wrong when Jerry tried to show his weaker nature. For her own good Jerry had to show that he was really a bit of a slob and he did this by being himself.

Poisonous never said much, but sometimes he said dead good things. He said women wanted to mould Jerry into whatever they wanted a man to be because Jerry seemed very mouldable. Poisonous said you can mould custard for ages, but it always ends up as custard.

And they hadn't had sex for six months before she threw him out. Jerry only stayed, he said, because she was sitting her finals at university that year and he didn't want the blame for anything that went wrong. But if he moved, it seemed he'd have to move in with me. Maybe not such an enticing prospect after all.

I was living on my own and I'd got used to it. I liked it. I laughed at the late-night weathermen and had a constant supply of beer. The grass plants had started to grow. I made my own bread. I didn't know how to when I moved in. I didn't know about baking bowls or baking tins. And I made soup. Apart from that there was sardines and vegetables and rice. I wasn't getting into any more debt. It was almost sustainable. If Jerry hadn't moved in, I could have had my girlfriend in the story and it could have been more like Mills & Boon. I only saw her at the weekends, anyway. The weekends can be a problem if you've no money, no pals, and no girlfriend. Jerry just didn't have a girlfriend. This unsettled me. Jerry always had a girlfriend. It would prey on my mind if he'd nothing to do at the weekend. I didn't want him to become lonesome.

I needn't have worried. The first weekend he brought home Louise. She was a nice girl, a student nurse who knew some of my ex-flatmates. Louise left her hairbrush. Later, she claimed that she hadn't screwed him anyway. But even later she worked in a massage parlour as one of the legions who tend to the laundry. It was hard to know with some people, but I took to her right away because she knew where to score speed.

Then there was Marty. She lived above me in South Clerk Street in a big flat full of junkies. I hadn't seen so much of her since I got evicted from there and having Jerry helped me to reacquaint myself. Marty was sixteen going on forty. She looked younger at twenty-nine than she had at sixteen. Her teeth were shot to hell, but she had other qualities. She was unusual. Marty left her hash pipe.

Living with Jerry immediately started costing me money. There were more opportunities to spend. You have to stay in practically all the time to crack the lonely financial zone. I started cooking his dinner for him when he got in, but Jerry wouldn't eat the sardines and brown rice and vegetables. We were back in mince and tattie land. This consumed some of the savings I made on the rent. The rest I spent on drugs. I had to get a bank loan. I told the bank manager my agent had assured me that big bucks were coming my way and could I have two hundred pounds please?

I didn't have an agent. I got the two hundred pounds, though. A couple of months later, the bank manager showed up at my door and asked for it back. Of course, I denied being me. Always gives one the high ground against men in suits, that. Can I speak to . . .? No, you can't.

I didn't know some of the people who came round. That first weekend this horrible person came to visit. He was straight out of central casting. A nightmare. The kind of person who gave drug dealing a bad name. He offered me a snort of speed so I had to pretend to be friendly, which made it even worse. Jerry had once introduced me to a person who had killed a man for his trousers. The bouncers wouldn't let him in wearing jeans. The fact that he was out of his nut on acid at the time didn't rehabilitate him in my eyes. I told Jerry that I didn't want to have any of these kinds of people coming round.

When it came to men, he lacked discrimination, but Jerry always went out with great-looking women. The first woman I ever saw him with was gorgeous. That's why Mora thought he was superman. She was two years older than Mora and one of the beautiful sixth-formers when Mora was still in fourth year. Jerry caught the glamour, but he really just wanted to go to his work, then come home and loaf around with a joint in his hand. He wanted to be comfortable in everything he did. He needed a woman to sit on the couch with him.

That's when I wheeled out Doreen. Doreen had lived in the South Clerk Street flat for about nine months before we got evicted. She'd been recommended by one of the original women, who then got into a slight morphine situation with Marty from upstairs and had to leave due to a sudden wallop of debt. Nobody offered her any help. The women stepped back as if she'd started to smell and then waved bye bye as she went back to mummy. Doreen then brought in her friend Tracy from the nurses' home.

Doreen was five ten and ten stone and knew how to look glamorous. It might take her hours, but she could do it. None of the women I knew could do that, or didn't want to, or thought it might be a bit off colour to tart yourself up like that anyway. Not Doreen. She'd paraded through the nightspots in Leeds and had managed to get men to give her things. When she was staying in South Clerk Street, sometimes she'd get them out and show them to you. This one gave her that, and this one gave her that, et cetera. Watches, bangles, baubles and beads. She was the closest thing to Zsa Zsa Gabor I was ever going to meet.

She had a boyfriend in the nurses' home then, and her English boyfriend, and there was this other guy she screwed sometimes. At least, that's what was going on when she stayed with me. For a little while I hadn't seen her after the break-up of the flat, but then she started unexpectedly visiting me. Sometimes she brought along

Tracy. I thought the break-up of the flat was acrimonious, but after a while it looked as if it was just me.

Before Jerry moved in, one night I was bringing him back from the boxing to give me a smoke when we found Doreen and Tracy waiting on the doorstep. They wanted to go dancing. At least Doreen did. It was Thursday night and they had the next day off. The fact that I'd no money, no job, no prospects, and didn't dance much didn't seem to matter. We ended up getting drunk in a club at the west end of Princes Street. Then Doreen wanted to show us the flat they'd moved into after the South Clerk Street débâcle.

We'd met the Tory councillor at the mental hospital and like a lot of these Tory bastards she seemed almost human and quite plausible. She was sorry but she couldn't show us the flat right then. I told her I worked in the City Libraries and she said she was my employer. I should have known then. We gave her the deposit and went to see the flat the next day. It was a room short. It was only going to fit three people. There were four of us, me and the three women. I was sitting in a room with the three of them and the atmosphere had a desperate feel to it. They hadn't been surfing the waves of anxiety which come with rented accommodation for long enough. The situation wasn't really that bad. We had a whole weekend to find somewhere else to live.

I grew bored sitting in the room with them. It needed someone to leave. One thing I'd learnt about the women I'd lived with in South Clerk Street was the merciless way they treated each other. At the first sign of a falter, a limp, a stumble along life's highway, they were out with the body bag and posting you back to the sticks before you could say 'Help'. The first one out the door got the knife in the back. I knew it. Doreen was being casual, as if it didn't really matter, and it didn't. Her pal Tracy just looked scared. I knew the Ice Woman would do it if I left the room, but I left anyway.

The Ice Woman called me out of bed to a flat meeting that night to tell me I wasn't moving in with them. I'd paid my money and signed a lease, and that's when it got acrimonious. The next day they moved into the flat and found the Tory bastard's husband living there. It was his flat. They'd split up, and moving in four people with him must have been his wife's idea of a joke. He shut the door in their faces. An hour later he shut the door in mine as well, after telling me what had happened. You've got to laugh.

The three of them moved temporarily into a flat owned by one of the Ice Woman's eunuch boyfriends. We must have had something else to drink after they took me and Jerry back there. I tried to get up from the couch and leave with Jerry, but I fell on to the floor instead. Rolling over and slowly getting to my knees. Doreen's got Jerry by the sleeve of his jacket and she's giving him a good yank, but he's getting away.

'Ooooh, come on. Stay, Jerry. Come on, stay,' she says. It's three in the morning and Jerry has to get up for his work at seven. He sometimes drove lorries into things. No wonder.

'Naw, Ah have tae go. Have tae go,' he says, not looking her directly in the face. She's got hold of his sleeve with both hands now.

'You can't go now, you can't,' says Doreen. 'I've got you and I'm not letting go.'

I rolled on to the couch. Tracy was sitting in one of the armchairs, not doing much of anything. Roars of laughter from Doreen as she lost her grip on the velvet jacket and fell on to her backside.

'That's it. Ah'm off, Matt. See ye,' says Jerry and staggers out the room.

But he's only got a ten-minute walk. Getting to Meadowbank would take me an hour if I could walk, which I couldn't. Not right then. People were trying to say things to each other amid the drunken disappointment on the floor behind the couch. I reeled about the room and battered off the door. No one was grabbing hold of me, forcing me to stay, but I didn't see how I could make it home.

'Ah'll have tae crash somewhere. Ah'm fucked. Where can Ah lie down?'

Doreen pointed me into a boxroom, the smallest in the flat. I was down to my simmit and was about to roll over and put the light out when Tracy stuck her head round the door, smiled broadly, said hullo, and then kind of jumped into the room.

Most young women look a lot better with fewer clothes on. She had beautiful breasts. They bounced towards me and the single bed I was lying on. Yellow knickers were all she was wearing. She seemed very pleased and happy and was not the drunken bum I was. I reeled back on the pillows as she came up from the foot of the bed.

I'd almost forgotten she was a virgin or perhaps imagined that she'd decided to slough off this state. No such luck. The knickers were staying on. A bit of wrestle ensued. I gave up the ghost as soon as she seemed determined. I couldn't believe it. What was she doing in the bed? What was I doing in the bed? Virgins. People pay extra to go to bed with virgins. That's weird. Drunk and

disgusted, I rolled over and almost immediately was
snoring.

Before I was twenty I wasted a lot of time trying to have
sex with virgins. I imagined one person I went out with
had to have her hymen surgically removed before her
wedding. Later on it was stretched and turned up as a
trampoline, part of a novelty act put on by a troupe of
midget gymnasts.

I felt awful in the morning. Shocked to see Tracy lying
there beside me in this narrow wee bed, I then concentrated for a bit on how I was gritting my teeth with that
kind of hangover which makes you feel tense and uptight
all over. Maybe it was just finding her in the bed. She
didn't jump up and run off. I'd forgotten it was her bed.
Of course, they would give the boxroom to Tracy. I asked
her about the night before and said I was sorry about the
wrestling.
   I started fondling her beautiful breasts. I didn't kiss her.
I just started groping her as if her body wasn't really part
of her or anybody else. It was like being able to climb
over the sculptures in an art gallery without anyone
checking you. Beautiful breasts. I slipped my hand down
her belly and into the yellow knickers. And she pulled it
back up. She didn't look at me, but looked a little miffed
without putting much conviction into it. I tried it again
and she pulled my hand back up on to her breasts again. It
seemed a bit comical.
   As I tried again, I started talking to her. Just matter-of-
fact stuff about her and this particular orifice. Was she all

right? Would it be all right? Did it have a hymen? No, it didn't. Not with two fingers jammed up her it didn't. Was she still a virgin? Yes, she still was. But without a hymen. Interesting. Perfect. I teased one of her feet out a bit and climbed on top of her. Even the knickers were perfect. Slackly elasticated, easily slipped past. I hadn't asked and she hadn't said no.

The erection was one of those hangover hard-ons which wasn't going to go away. Her hole was unlike other holes. Maybe it was just how sensitive the top of my cock was, but the grip was perfect as I slowly but so slowly guided it up her. I was just in by the knob when a thought jumped into my head.

'Ah'm goiny to stick it right up ye!' I thought.

So with my teeth clenched and grimacing, I gave her the whole thing in one swift push past folds and curtains of resistance I did not recognise. She looked as if she'd been stabbed at first, the way her mouth and her eyes gawped simultaneously. Then she started to bellow:

'Get off! Get off me! Oh, no! Oh, no! Get off!'

At the same time she started pushing at my hips in an attempt to climb up the bed and off my cock. I don't know what I was saying at the time to try and pacify her, but it wasn't working. I moved my hips once or twice, or tried to despite the squirming, but that nearly brought on hysterics. I rolled off and gave a big sigh. She wouldn't know what to do with my cock to make the moment any better and, besides, suddenly I felt awful again.

I stumbled off looking for the toilet, the erection feeling a little uncomfortable against the fabric of my jeans. Doreen was probably still sleeping in a big double bed somewhere. I wondered if I should go and find her, and ask her for some help with this erection. She was a friend of mine, and I thought if she was tired and sleepy she might give me a quiet ride without thinking too much about it. But she'd probably be even worse hung over than me.

⸺⸺⸺⸺⸺⸺

When I was a young person, *Lady Chatterley's Lover* was banned. We didn't talk about fucking people, or shagging people, or riding people. We talked about having it off. When I went to university, I heard the middle-class Prods I started hanging out with talking about screwing people. To them, talking about shagging or fucking anyone was definitely non-U. You hear a lot of young people talking about shagging and fucking and riding people these days. Something's happened. Whatever it was, I can now write about sex and use these words and nobody's really going to mind. You can still make love if you like. Even then, the person you're doing it with might be fucking you. Hard to tell. Let's take the liberty of using all these words and differentiate by way of motivation.

⸺⸺⸺⸺⸺⸺

Jerry had decided he wasn't going to go to bed with Doreen that night, not because he was going to work the next day, but because he was still living with Mora. Even though he wasn't having sex with Mora. That's the kind of guy Jerry was. He wanted to do the right thing. I could not understand this. He'd been brought up with all the normal moral education of the usual Scottish heathen and I never understood how some non-Catholics would behave the way Jerry did that night. Where did he get such values from? He must have invented them himself. Jerry was the kind of guy you'd never hear talking about fucking, riding, or shagging anyone.

But if you live for a while with a group of good-looking, relatively unattached young women who are not your relatives, it is easy to sink into a seeping miasma of lechery. Though I was brought up to view the Virgin Mary as the ultimate female ideal, I did imagine how much I would enjoy doing things to Doreen quite often. But I realised it would not come for free. Something about Doreen made you think you might have to take the whole package. She looked as if she could pack a fair wallop as well.

She knew she was there to get off with Jerry when she showed up at the flat that night, months later. She'd been cued. She brought along her friend Tracy. We went to the pub. We drank home brew. We smoked dope. The jealous monster stayed perched on my shoulder. Doreen told Tracy to stay the night. She agreed. No one asked me. Tracy got drunk, grew suddenly hysterical and fled into the night. I never said a word. I rolled up the last bit of dope. Doreen was lying, maybe sleeping, maybe not, on the folded-down green, foam-filled settee. I looked over at Doreen. I looked at Jerry.

'Ah suppose Ah'd better go tae bed,' I said.

'Ah suppose so,' said Jerry. He smiled winningly.

You really have to do something with a man in order to get some bonding organised, something that doesn't involve women. Sitting around smoking dope with them isn't quite what I mean. You've got to play golf, or darts, or go to the football, or get punched in the head together. We'd become closer due to going to the boxing. But we weren't getting punched in the head by the time he got

off with Doreen. We were still hitting bags and trying to
get fit.

I'd put on at least a stone in weight due to my ulcer.
Sometimes I had to eat every two hours, even through
the night. I hadn't taken any exercise since I was eighteen.
By the time I was twenty-five I knew I'd better do something before I went so far down the hill that I couldn't
get back up it again. Watching the TV at night, I taught
myself how to skip, more or less. I could do ten press-ups
when I walked into the Meadowbank Stadium with Jerry.

There isn't really any winning and losing in sparring.
There's better or worse. Every time I went to the club I'd
watch the sparring, though I'd never actually stand and
stare at it. You didn't really do that. I used to watch it,
though. It was scary. It was hard to imagine at first what
it was like to do that.

Kids would spar while the rest of us did skipping and
press-ups and stuff like that. When you were hot and
broken up, you were supposed to get gloved up and spar.
That's when me and Jerry would politely make excuses
and stick to hitting the bags. We didn't have to make
excuses. It looked at first as if we'd get killed if we tried
to spar with these people. I was still trying to learn how to
throw a straight left and a straight right.

This can in time lead to bewildering combinations of
lefts and rights, such as left right, right left, and left left
right. It is the basis of boxing and can be practised in the
privacy of your own home. But once you have mastered
the rudiments of throwing a left and a right in the Meadowbank Boxing Club, you are left taking sidelong glances
at the boxing ring.

The trainer, Bill, said the sparring at that time hadn't

been so good for years. The club had produced the best amateur lightweight in Britain. The Scottish amateur light heavyweight champion trained there. They had five junior champions all about to move into the seniors. And they seemed to knock the seven shades of shite out of each other every night I was there. It was so fast and whole-hearted. I knew I was about to ask to participate in this. I'd been going to the club for several months and I kept putting off asking because I knew they'd let me. I was about to volunteer. Jerry was back in the flat nursing a head cold. No one would witness my possibly grotesque humiliation.

Wee Benny looked like a sparrow. He was chirpy and cheerful, even though his face did look as if it had been hit by a shovel several times.

'Aye, son,' he said. 'Ye can spar if ye want.'

He asked if I'd a gumshield. I said no. It hadn't occurred to me. He curled back my lip and asked if my teeth were long. My teeth are exceptionally long. 'They're okay,' he said. I already had on a pair of sixteen-ounce gloves. Someone had tied them up for me before I went over to the ring. Wee Benny told me to sit down.

There's a raised plank along the wall. The ring is eighteen inches in front of your face. When bodies come careering backwards across the ring and slam into the ropes, you can practically lean forward and bite their bums. I'm sitting down beside the best amateur light-weight in Britain. I can hardly contain my nervousness.

'Whit's it like?' I said, just to say something.

'It's no like hittin' bags,' he said. 'People hit back.'

People at the boxing would always talk to you. They were quite friendly. Other Scottish people describe Edinburgh people as cold, but it's really middle-class Edinburgh people they're talking about. It might even be middle-class people who stay in Edinburgh, because a great many people who stay in the middle of the town don't come from here. I don't come from here. I only know one person from Edinburgh and I've lived here over twenty years. Middle-class people in this town will cut you dead, but not all of them are Scottish. Most of them are English. Middle-class English people might be more fucked up than Scottish middle-class people because they have even less sense of community. They've never spoken to their neighbours. They come from families where parents might retire to places full of people they don't know. The centre of Edinburgh in many ways resembles an English town, but all the people I met at the boxing came from the outer reaches where the working-class people live. The working-class people in Edinburgh are the same as the working-class people from the West of Scotland except that they've never won anything. But they're friendly and all kinds of quips and badinage might occur between punches to the head.

The light heavyweight was sparring as I sat down on the wooden plank. Five other people were sitting on the plank and the light heavyweight sparred with them all, except me, twice. He also sparred with one or two other people. Basically, he sparred with everyone who was gloved up. The last person he sparred with was the lightweight I was sitting beside. People are divided into different weights in boxing because big guys tend to beat up wee guys. But the only person in the gym that the lightweight could really unload on was the light heavyweight. The three-stone difference in weight sometimes didn't look big enough. The lightweight seemed to be swarming all over him. Good sparring was what Bill, who usually ran the sparring, wanted and he always put the lightweight in when the light heavy was a bit tired. It was like Popeye and Pluto.

When the light heavy had done a minute of this, Bill let him out and waved me in. It wasn't as if he was going to put me in with anyone I'd any chance of beating. But they could all have beaten me. They could all have beaten me up.

'A minute,' he said. 'Fast an' light!'

Everyone knows the story about the guy off the street who steps into the ring with the world champ and knocks him flat on his bum. We've all seen the movie. It's not true, but there's a way that it might be. If you're sparring with an orthodox boxer, he's going to lead with his left. That's what makes him an orthodox boxer. A southpaw is going to stand with his right foot forward and lead with his right. You know these things as the other boxer shapes up in front of you. A southpaw who leads with his left is going to miss and should get hit for it. So he's going to lead with his right. Who knows what somebody who knows nothing about boxing is going to do? Probably rush headlong and flail the air like a complete lunatic. It is just conceivable that this person might surprise the world champion and hit him flat on his bum. No one ever tells you what happens when the world champion gets up.

I bore down on the best amateur lightweight in Britain and I was wide-eyed. It had taken weeks and weeks to get myself geed up for this. I was bursting with fear and tension and I didn't want to be crying in the corner after the first ten seconds. All I knew was that I had to go forward and try to throw straight lefts and rights. He moved back as I moved forward. For an instant he seemed to be waiting for something and then I threw a left which went through his guard and scuffed his cheek.

'He hit him! He hit him!' Wee Benny shouted from the side of the ring. He was amazed, not that I'd knocked Wee John, as the lightweight was known, on his bum, but that I'd connected with him at all.

Wee John backed towards the corner, went off the rope to my left, bounced off the ropes to my right and landed a left hook flush on my chin. The last time someone had hit me was a long, long time before and no one had ever hit me like that. Everything went brilliant white, then black, then white. Normal service was returned in an instant.

I hadn't fallen or stumbled, or anything like that. I blundered forward. I held my hands up. I threw lefts in Wee John's general direction. Without knowing it, I was hassling him. He was going to have to hit me again. Whack! Another left hook. Pure sky blue, stars falling from the upper peripherals.

I don't think I was ever hit as hard as that in sparring ever again. And I didn't fall. My knees didn't buckle. My legs didn't feel like jelly. He'd obviously missed. Not as much as I did. I missed him for the next minute, then Bill called time. And told Wee John to get out. I was dying after a minute. And he told Wee John to get out. I couldn't believe it. I had to spar with someone else!

Didn't hit much there either. Then I was out. Then back in and out again. Then back in again. I ended up following the light heavyweight around. He'd taken pity on me and decided not to kill me after all. Thud, thud.

Just the occasional straight left to the frontal lobes. I'd never been tireder. Bill set me free after I'd sparred for a total of six minutes. My skeleton alone seemed to hold me up in the wonderful Meadowbank showers. All my muscles seemed deadened, tired, glowing.

Jerry didn't have to ask me if I'd been sparring. I knew where my nose and cheeks were without having to think about it. But it was my lips that told the story. They were bruised and broken, swollen a little. That's why you have to wear a gumshield. It's not to keep your teeth in your head after all, though that's handy. For some reason it saves your lips. I don't know how. Take it from me. It does.

We both bought gumshields and next week Jerry went into the ring. I thought he was the bravest man in the world. The way the blows thudded off him made me want to look away. But that's what happens when you don't know what you're doing. You're so tense you don't go with the blows. Hitting someone like that is like hitting a plank of wood. There's no give. You can practically see the brain reverberating.

But didn't we feel much better for it in the pub later on. We'd both seen the white light, looked into the blackness, seen the stars. No one we knew was as crazy as we were. We laughed out loud.

Jerry wasn't laughing a couple of weeks later. He'd come in from his work and found me at the table in the middle of the living room. This was unusual since I usually worked in the bedroom these days. But I was out of my nut on speed. I must have looked mad, staring over at him as he came in and slumped down on the couch. Papers were all over the floor. I'd hardly moved since he'd gone to work that morning. But Jerry must have expected me to look like that. I didn't expect him to look the way he did. He was grey. His gob was somewhat ajar. He'd just been to the bog. He hadn't looked as bad as that when he came home.

'You look fuckin' awful,' said I, the speed freak. He didn't respond. 'Whit's up?' I said

'Ah think Ah've got the clap,' he said slowly.

chapter three

〜〜〜〜〜〜〜

My jaw dropped. Never was much use in a crisis. 'How did ye get that?' said I.

I didn't want to ask what it was like. A friend of a friend once had the clap and there were mutters about green drips, so I felt it best not to inquire. Jerry thought he might have a doctor take a look at it, but he didn't have one. I gave him mine. Because of my ulcer, she kept asking for pieces of faecal matter to investigate, but didn't mind when I kept shaking my head. Jerry went straight down. He told her he thought he had the clap and she told him to go to the clap clinic.

I had to phone up for him since he couldn't from his work the next day. He was seeing Doreen that Friday and was in a hurry to know. So I phoned them up and told them I had the clap and could I have an appointment, please? They weren't going to give me one the next day. My willie could have been dropping off for all they knew. I told them I'd caught it off an American tourist who was leaving town the next night, but they sounded as if they'd heard that one before.

When Jerry finally got to see them, they told him he had the clap. They also told him it took three weeks to incubate and he'd have to contact anyone he'd poked over this period and ask them to come for a check-up, please.

So we worked it out on the floor that night. He'd have to tell Louise, Marty and Doreen. Doreen would have to tell both her other boyfriends and the other guy she sometimes screwed. The ramifications were mind-boggling. We ended up with a list of thirteen people. Marty had gone to Mull and we wouldn't be able to get hold of her for a couple of weeks. We thought he must have caught it off Marty. We just assumed it was him to blame for infecting Doreen. Somehow you don't expect glamorous, fragrant people to go around spreading the clap.

She was coming round that Friday night. It was her twenty-first birthday. He'd bought her a watch. She asked what I was smirking about, then they went out for a drink. Jerry had orange juice. The conversation went something like this.

'Why are ye havin' orange juice, Jerry?'

'Ah'm no allowed tae drink on the penicillin.'

'Have you got summit the matter?'

'Ah'm afraid so.'

'Is it serious?'

'Yeah. Ah've got the clap.'

'But that's no so bad . . . *Oh my God!*'

She had to sneak away from her training to attend the clinic.

When she was coming out, she met Louise going in. Louise said she'd never even screwed the guy in too loud a voice. Doreen had to run like hell down the corridor when her classmates appeared round the corner.

A month or so later we bumped into the guy she sometimes screwed. He asked after her. We said she'd left town. He said that was a pity. I asked if he wasn't bothered about catching the clap off her. He said he'd had the clap six times. Marty said her results were clean.

Of course, if you caught the clap from unprotected sex these days, you'd be almost bound to ask the girl out again. What a nice girl! She just gave me the clap.

It didn't go down so well with the Scottish boyfriend. Doreen had told him about Jerry before Jerry had told her about the clap. She hadn't told the Scottish boyfriend yet. A bit delicate. Sorry our love didn't work out. Here's the number for the clap clinic, by the way. We were all at a party the next Saturday. The Scottish boyfriend was drinking too much and walking around with a glower on. He accused me of something at one point, but I, of course, denied all knowledge. At the end of the night, he was staring balefully at a girl who was sitting alone in a corner. The last one left. He looked disgruntled and walked slowly across the room. Here comes Mister Disease. How's about a big clap?

The poor bastard got a secondary infection called Writer's Syndrome. Maybe it's Righter's or Ritter's. Anyway, he was crawling around on his hands and knees for a while before they hospitalised him. Swollen joints. Arthritic thingies. The anonymous wallflower got away with just the usual course of antibiotics.

I had a job a year or so later which involved filing British Standards. Your kettle might be made to a British Standard, the British Standard for kettles. To protect the consumer. If they're changing the standard, they'll tell you why. I had to replace the old British Standards by new ones. A new one came up for condoms. You can file British Standards for quite a while and not get a laugh. They were adding a colour-fastness test for condoms because the customers had started using ones that were black or were adorned with the Stars and Stripes, etc. They must have added a flavour test by this time.

~~~~~~~~~~~~~~~

You couldn't get condoms in Edinburgh when I came here in 1969. Well, you could ask at a chemist. Nobody did. You could get them from a barber, but that was a bit tricky if the hair was half-way down your back. There was a surgical supply store at the back of Woolworth's in Princes Street and people used to go in there. Condoms wear out, of course, if you keep them in your ticket pocket for a year and a half. The paper foil comes off them and then you have to go and get another one.

~~~~~~~~~~~~~~~

If we'd had condoms kicking around, Jerry would still have caught the clap. We didn't keep condoms in the flat because we didn't use them. Everyone we knew was on the pill. We didn't know any virgins except for Tracy.

Tracy was from a village half-way between Glasgow and Edinburgh and I think Doreen felt a bit guilty about leaving her in the nurses' home when she left for South Clerk Street. Tracy had somehow managed to get under Doreen's wing, probably by appearing not to be too smart. So Tracy moved to South Clerk Street and it's hard to imagine what it must be like to leave home, have a brief sojourn in a nurses' home and then move into a place like that flat. For one thing, she didn't have to pay any rent or bills. When we got the eviction notice, I refused to pay any bills, calculating that we wouldn't be cut off before we reached the bum's rush date. So there she landed, no bills, no rent, no support and weird people all over the place.

There weren't any virgins there except Tracy. The other women sometimes took the piss. Maybe that's what you're supposed to do when you leave home. Get somewhere weird to live and lose your virginity if you've still got it. Maybe that's why Doreen kept pushing her into bed with me. Maybe Doreen just wanted to have someone around to catch the bus with the next day. I didn't know. She just showed up at the flat one night with Tracy. Stay, Tracy, stay. Go on. Just stay the night. Sitting there, saying nothing, watching this is a bit odd.

When I got into the bed, Tracy was still awake. I told her if you went to bed with males, you had to deal with erections. There was no point in ignoring them. It was a trade-off. If you didn't want to be screwed, you had to pull or suck. Erections will not go away, I said. If you leave them there, you will get nothing but aggravation. Then I told her that everything was okay because I was too drunk to be bothered and just wanted to go to sleep.

In the morning she was still there. I went to the bog and came back. She was still there. There was nowhere else to go, since Jerry and Doreen weren't up yet. Beautiful breasts. Hung over, but not sick or anything. Nothing else to do really. Beautiful breasts. She had a hold of my cock. The kind of thing which would make you want to sit up and take notice if you weren't better off lying down. Nobody had said anything. I started a do-this, do-that conversation. You could tell somehow that she'd never held one before. I slipped my hand down her body and into her knickers. They looked the same as the last time. Yellow, crêpy stuff. She was wet. My other hand was over her hand since she didn't really have the action sussed then. Suddenly, a thought came into my head.

'Ah might as well jist fuck ye!' I thought.

I never asked her. I'd never been with anyone before and never asked. I just climbed on top of her and asked her to open her legs wider. She did. I started guiding it in very slowly, talking to her quietly all the time. I don't think I needed to bother. She was looking to the side the way people sometimes do when you haven't done it with them before.

That always pisses me off. Why do they look to the side as if you're not there any more? Or they're not there. Maybe they think it's nothing to do with them. Maybe it's the start of divorcing yourself from the situation. Okay, I'll leave it here and you can fuck it while I look out the window. How are you supposed to make love to someone who avoids looking at your face?

'That's it right up ye,' I said. 'Can you feel it throbbin'?'

She looked at me then. 'Yes,' she said.

'That's it goin' out. An' that's it goin' back in,' I said. 'Have ye ever done this before?'

'No.'

'Well, I'll make it quick,' I said.

I was still half waiting for her to freak out and start screaming blue murder, but she just slotted her head to the side again. I was resting my weight on my hands and soon had built up a nice, steady, fast rhythm. Suddenly, another idea jumped into my head.

'This is better than a wank,' I thought.

Her beautiful tits were bouncing in time. I was banging her to watch the effect. Her head started waving about a bit from side to side. Her face went a bit red. Her eyes developed a very vague look to them as if she wasn't quite there.

This can happen to you when you get punched in the head. Repeated blows to the head, none of which might be enough to knock you down, make you fall into the abyss, the blackness, the whiteness, the stars, sometimes give you a feeling of great detachment. It's as if you lose contact almost with your body. You have a vague unease, a feeling that you should maybe do something, but you don't really mind. It's a bit like floating unsteadily on your feet. Time for a standing count.

It's as close as I can get to what was happening to Tracy. She was going to the moon. Only something very bad happening would jerk her back to earth. She'd lost it completely. Though she was doing nothing, she was out of control. She was lying flat on her back getting her tits bounced around. I was doing it. She was getting it done to her. I was active. I was in control.

I'd got to the point where I was looking at the wall and trying to stay in control. Another thought jumped into my head.

'Why don't ye jist let her have it?'

Endgame. I was banging her at top speed, gritting my teeth, when I suddenly pulled out of her and pumped spunk all over her belly button. I was still supporting

myself on my hands. I might have said something like
'Uh'.

'Look at that! Look at that! Look what you've done to
me!' she screeched. She pressed the palms of her hands
down into the bed and stared down at the spunk in horror.
She'd obviously never seen spunk before. Maybe she
thought it was a pool of milky snotters. That's the way
she was acting. I slumped on to my face by her side. I'd
forgotten about the hangover. 'Look at it! Look at it!' she
said, but I don't think she was really speaking to me.

I read a book by a psychologist once who said if you didn't
do it right, you got screwed up. Practically no one did it
right and that was why the world was screwed up. I
assumed he was talking about men. Phallocentric psychologist says men are fucked up. Coitus interruptus, he
said, fucks up your head. He might have added that
fathering children fucks up your head as well.

I sat on the couch a short while after getting out of bed
that morning and I didn't feel as if I'd got something. I
felt as if I'd lost something. I was dressed in a lab coat I'd
stolen a couple of years before, sipping tea. Jerry was
rolling a stick and neither of us was saying much. Doreen
rushed in from the lobby where she'd been speaking to
Tracy.

'Tracy said you screwed her!' she said. I saw Tracy out
in the hall behind her, just about to go back into the
bedroom. She looked radiantly happy. I did not understand any of it. But I was just sparring with her then. It
wasn't like that a while later.

I only saw two people getting beat up in sparring and I was one of them. It shouldn't happen. The first time I saw it happen, it happened to an American guy.

He was the worst kind of American guy. He showed up at the gym and wanted to spar. There he was, sitting on the bench between me and the welterweight called Jim. The American started shouting and pointing into the ring.

'Look, he's holding back!' he shouted. 'He could have hit him there! He could have hit him! Look, he's pulling back!'

Jim the Welterweight told the boy that Wee John, the best amateur lightweight in the country, had to pull back, but the boy wouldn't listen.

'Look, he's pulling back again!' said this American guy excitedly.

Totally uncool is the only way to describe it. The American guy had done some martial arts training somewhere, but he didn't even know enough to be scared when he sat down on that raised plank. Bill the Trainer called him into the ring and let him spar with someone who was even worse at boxing than me. The American boy did not seem to understand the words 'fast and light'. The trainer called Jim the Welterweight in. Jim the Welterweight was only seventeen. He was beautiful at seventeen. If he'd been living near the Kronk gym in Detroit, he could have been a contender. Jim the Welterweight did not pull back on the American boy. I was watching Bill the Trainer and wondering how long he was going to leave the American boy in there. The boy's nose was burst. There was a bit of blood. I thought it might be time to get the gloves off and hit some bags instead. The American boy never showed up again. I sparred with Jim the Welterweight later and he was all right with me.

It was the flyweight who beat me up. I'd been sparring, it seemed, for ages by then and that night I'd done a couple of minutes already. I felt wonderful that night. I wasn't scared. I was beginning to relax into it. I felt really sharp and light on my feet. I went back in against Danny the Flyweight. When you're with someone about a foot smaller than you and three stone lighter, who just happens to be twice as fit and ten times better at boxing than you, you tend to try to keep them at arm's length. You jab and move. People with shorter arms get hit first and then try to get inside to pound on your ribs. Long arms aren't much use against short arms inside.

But you don't know what it feels like when you hit the other guy. You can imagine it later, but you only really know what it's like when you get hit. Instead of throwing out a jab and moving back, which was how me and Danny the Flyweight normally sparred, I felt so full of myself that I jabbed and stayed there. When he came in, I hit him again. That was two punches he'd taken on the forehead. I hit him the third time and got him annoyed.

Danny the Flyweight later fought for the British professional title. He was only seventeen or eighteen then, but he'd been boxing since he was twelve or so. I began to cast glances at the trainer then. It was not Bill. Bill was off. That night George was taking the sparring. George the Trainer did not know what it was like to spar or get punched in the head at all. He'd never boxed. He'd said a minute when I got in the ring, but if it was a minute it was a very long one.

Danny the Flyweight gave a demonstration of body punching. If you're three stone lighter, you don't have to hold back. Body punching is sickening. There's no other way to describe it. It takes away all your strength. It makes your arms drop. You don't get any visuals. You just get depressed. Bang, bang, bang. I couldn't keep him away. I kept looking at the trainer. Had his watch stopped? Why didn't he get me out of there?

'Thuck dis!' I said. People always say things like that when they're wearing a gumshield.

You know when someone's stopped. You know when someone's given in. The set of their body just goes. They could be standing on the street. I got out of the ring and pulled off the gloves. I was pissed off with the trainer. I was pissed off with myself. I was pissed off with everyone. I put on some training mitts and started hitting a heavy bag. Jim the Welterweight came over. He stood close to my back, laughing in my ear.

'Ah knew that was going happen! Ah knew it!' he said. 'Once Ah saw you hittin' him like that, Ah knew he'd go raj, ken? Ah knew it.'

'Ah wish you'd fuckin' told me,' I said.

You sometimes have to try and remember that this sparring stuff is not about beating people up. There is a silent agreement between people who spar together a lot. They know just how dominant one or other of them is going to be. They spar almost as if they've developed a routine. And the cardinal rule is that you don't take liberties. You dish it out and you soak it up, but if you take liberties the people you rely on to spar with will start finding excuses for not sparring with you. Either that or they'll stand there and beat the crap out of you.

Because Jerry was sparring and I was sparring and everyone had to spar with everyone else, I had to spar with Jerry. You have to try to remember it's not personal. Jerry and I had no excuses for not sparring with each other, so we ponced about and made it look like the kind of sparring you might see sometimes on TV. We didn't land many blows. We made it look as if we were working when we were shirking really. When Jerry and I were sparring, the sparring was crap.

After a wee while, I didn't want to hit him. We weren't competitive really because it soon became obvious that I was going to be much better at boxing than Jerry. Jerry would have made a better wrestler than me. As a kid, he'd played rugby and not football and maybe that's why he never looked light and mobile on his feet. This meant that when Jerry wanted to make contact, you weren't there. When you wanted to make contact, he couldn't get away. Jerry could only stalk you, and when he did catch up with you you usually had to batter him one. This made Jerry the bravest person in the whole gym. Every time he went to the boxing, he went into the ring. He never shirked it. He said it was the only way to learn. Sometimes I had to look away.

When I started sparring Wee Benny gave me a book called *Boxing Teaches a Boy*. It was really a pamphlet published in the 1920s. The author in one night won *three* Scottish amateur titles. He didn't have to box just three times to do this. He had to box his way through the preliminaries at each weight and had fought *nine* fights by the time he was finished. They had to cut his gloves off at the end of the night, due to his hands swelling up. What a guy! My hero! He said in the book that you had to do road work. There was no way out of it. 'Braving the grins and stares of passers-by', it said. Even fifty years later the pavements weren't full of joggers. I don't think jogging was even a word then. I don't think trainers was a word either. You certainly couldn't buy them in the shops for poncing about street corners, looking cool. The author of the book recommended running in army boots. I braved the grins and stares in a pair of old gutties. Running for ages on pavements in gutties is bound to fuck up every joint in your body eventually, but at first it was all I had. Jerry had a pair of baseball boots.

'Kill yourself on the roads,' Wee Benny said. Jerry ran like a tank. He could hit a pace and stick with it. I followed him some of the way round Arthur's Seat and then he followed me for a bit, and then I followed him. First one back got to shower first. But it didn't matter who was first or second. Both of us spent hours afterwards staring at the walls in numbed exhaustion.

By the time we started running, everything had settled down a bit. Jerry and I were living amicably in the wee flat. Doreen had stopped screwing around after catching the clap. Tracy had even got herself a boyfriend. I'd finished two drafts of the novel about the steelworks and was working on another one which was eventually published nine years later. Everything was chugging along rather nicely and then Mora started to show up.

chapter four

～～～～～～～

We didn't have a telephone. I'd only lived in a flat with a telephone once before. People just arrived or didn't. You were usually glad to see them unless they were the bank manager or the men with the big antennae asking if you had a television licence.

～～～～～～～

Once I opened the flat door and there were two men in overcoats standing there. One was holding a clipboard. The door to the living room was open and, by then, three black-and-white TVs were stacked up in a corner. All of them were on, but only one had the sound up. The man with the clipboard asked me if I had a TV. I said no. He ticked the sheet on his clipboard, said thank you, and went away. Just say no. It's what you get taught at school, the one lesson never to forget. It wisnae me. Blanket denial. If I'd admitted to having even one TV, I might have got myself into a bit of trouble there.

～～～～～～～

I bought my first TV licence after the BBC gave me some money for a radio play. It's a definite marker on the descent into respectability. I got money for a radio play because I met a writer. He was my first writer and I met him after I'd been writing in a compulsive, obsessive fashion for about eight years. I hadn't sold a word.

He was the typical writer. He'd had an asthmatic childhood spent mostly at home in bed. His dad had been an undertaker. He used to sit with the body-stuffers among the coffins. They showed him how to play cards and told him about premature burials. He had the nightmares for ever. He was still getting them when I met him, anyway. By then his dad had died and he lived up a tower block with his mum. He wrote and played himself at darts. His ambition when I came across him was to get a permanent job before he was thirty. He was twenty-nine.

It was in a cataloguing room at Napier College, now a uni. He was wittering on to anyone who would listen about how he might not need a permanent job if he could sell this radio play to the BBC. He said he was looking for an agent. I was fascinated. All writers do it. They puff themselves up. They have to broadcast it. I'm not just a pathetic little wanker who has to sit on his own for hours every day. I'm a writer.

Some people will even go to see them reading. Not only can the kid write, he can read too. Very badly. Sometimes stuff should be read out, but maybe it should be read out by actors. Celebrity, even minor, minor celebrity, has a weird effect on people. If you get your name in the papers, people will come and see you reading, especially if you'll do material that's about humping other people, or fiddling with yourself, and has lots of swear-words. That's the kind of stuff that I've enjoyed going to see over the past few years anyway, since I decided I was so out on a limb I'd better go and see what writers looked like. I met my first writer when I was about thirty and started being friendly with one or two when I began to creep up on my forties. They said that reading in public is a good way to get your hole. Sad but true. Maybe good and true. They come and see you acting like a performing monkey and then they let you perform all over them.

About the time I was living with Jerry, people used to ask me what I was going to do. As in, what are you going to do with yourself? Better-dressed, patronising bastards sometimes ask you this when you're a certain age. I used to tell them I was going to be a famous writer. Stare them in the face and say I'm going to be a famous writer. Holds them up a bit. If they're confident in themselves, they might stick around long enough to ask what kind of things you write. Words. It's the only answer. But if they ever ask you where you get your ideas from, you should tell them to go fuck themselves. Because if you ever tell people you're a writer, you're going to hear a lot of that one.

I don't know why Mora started coming round. Maybe she'd nowhere else to go. A short while after Jerry was chucked out, Mora sold her dad's medium-sized flat and he bought her the usual wee flat in Stockbridge. Poisonous went off to live with his girlfriend. It was maybe then, with the university business concluded, and the summer job finishing up, and the living alone, that she reckoned things had been better before. Maybe it was finding out about Doreen. We heard nothing from her for a couple of months after Jerry moved his stuff out. Then Poisonous told her about Doreen and she showed up at the flat one day.

Poisonous used to do things like that. Tell people things when it would have been better to keep his trap shut. He did it to me. Once, when he was drunk, he told my girlfriend that I'd been sleeping with someone. This was true. I had been sleeping with someone. What he failed to mention was that I'd been sleeping with this someone ten years earlier. He did it to Jerry as well. Soon after Jerry got him the room in Marchmont, when he was drunk, he told Mora that Jerry was still sleeping with his ex-girlfriend as well as occasionally still sleeping with the girl they'd been sharing a flat with. The reason why Poisonous did these things was because he was a poisonous little bastard. You could say he was a deep, dear friend and a poisonous little bastard as well.

I realised later that Mora was one of the few women I knew at the time that I didn't have sexual fantasies about. When a sexual fantasy about Mora began to cross my mind, I quickly got rid of it. It would have been like having a sexual fantasy about your kid sister. It's just not one of the roads you want to go down. To me, Mora was one of the wonderful people. I didn't know all that many people, but I thought they were all wonderful, though this usually required intoxicants or narcotics of some kind to be convincing. You had to wish it as well. But I thought Mora was one of the wonderful people all right.

Her grandfather had been a working-class hero, a

founder member, a blacklistee. Her parents were both professional middle-class people who got divorced as soon as the kids left home. Teachers at Mora's school expected great things of her. She had brains in spades, not that it showed up in her university finals, but by then she had complications to contend with, like living with Jerry and Poisonous and, at one time, me. She'd given me a room when I got back to Edinburgh a couple of years after leaving university. I owed her a lot. I liked her a lot. When she fell out with Jerry, she didn't just disappear, or go abroad. She was connected to some of the people we knew because a lot of these people had gone to the same high school in Stirling. It was through them that she'd got off with Jerry in the first place.

I was surprised to see her standing there. Her flat didn't have a shower and she said she needed to use ours. God, it was awful to see her standing there asking to use our shower. She looked terrible. I asked her to come in. I made her a cup of tea. She sat kind of hunched on one of the armchairs, and rubbed her nose, and looked at the ground. Then she started to weep, the shoulders shuddering, the whole bit.

The last time something like that had happened to me, it was Marty from the junkie flat upstairs in South Clerk Street. She was standing in the middle of my floor early one evening, shaking and trying to squeeze out the words. She'd been out to score some smack and the four guys there had gang-banged her after she jacked up. So this horrible story is starting to unfold in small stages and she's shaking and everything, and there was bugger all I could do about it. There was nothing anybody could do about it. You couldn't go to the police, supposing you wanted to, with a story like that. That's one of the reasons why everything should be legalised. If someone rips you off in a dope scene, the only thing you can do is forget about it, or take matters into your own hands, or pay someone else to. Stanley knives and baseball bat time. With Marty, she just had to tell someone and I suppose I just happened to be available. But I was hopeless and helpless. I couldn't even put my arms round her.

I think I've still got problems with touch. If you've got kids, maybe they help you get over it with all the hugging and everything. Back in 1977, I only put my arms round a woman if I was expecting to have sex with her. So when women I wasn't expecting to have sex with and had never had sex with before wept in front of me, there wasn't a lot I could do. I just stood there and felt more and more uptight. Being wired up like that made you want to punch the wall. I tried to sit down and listen and drink the tea instead.

Mora said she hadn't chucked him out at all. She only wanted some space to do her exams and then she was going to sell her dad's flat and move with Jerry into the usual wee flat. This wasn't true, but she managed to convince herself that it was gospel. I found this difficult to come to terms with. I kept thinking to myself that she must know in some way that this wasn't true, that somewhere inside her she must realise she was making all this crap up. But she didn't. She'd worked out some kind of scenario which helped explain her current unhappiness and that was that.

It was all Doreen's fault. Mora asked if Jerry had been sleeping with Doreen while he was still staying in Marchmont. I told her this definitely wasn't true. She obviously

didn't believe me. I told her that I knew for certain he
wasn't sleeping with Doreen then. I could see she still
didn't believe me. Doreen had to have stolen Jerry away.
It was the only construction on her past that would satisfy
her. It was all Doreen's fault.

I found that very hard to cope with. Especially in the
afternoon. Weeping and wailing and complaining in the
late afternoon. I just let her talk and gave her something
to wipe away the bitter tears. It was horrible seeing
someone so unhappy. It made me jumpy, on edge. She
said she was going to get Jerry back. It just wasn't fair. It
wasn't fair. I told her Jerry would be home from his work
soon and she went for a shower.

'Who's in the shower?' says Jerry.

'Mora,' I replied, kind of rolling my eyes.

'Whit's she doin' here?' he asked, alarmed a little.

'Ah'm goin' fur a run,' I said, making for the shallow
living-room cupboard where we kept the running gear.
'She's been here fur a couple of hours.'

'What's up?' says Jerry.

'Ah think she's goin' mad,' I said.

I got dressed quickly and, braving the grins and stares
of passers-by, went for a run round Arthur's Seat.

~~~~~~~~~~~~~~~~~~~~~~

That's how my first radio play started. A guy was running
round Arthur's Seat. I'd written three or four novels by
that time, but I knew I wasn't going to get any of them
published. I did not feel connected to whatever it is you
have to be connected to. So I wrote a few scenes of a play,
a comedy about a nurse losing his job through getting
bust with almost enough dope to get lost up your right
nostril. It was a true story. The bust cost him his job, but
he was on the dole for four years afterwards so it cost

everyone else as well. Anyway, after I met my first writer, I joined up the scenes with monologues and sent it in to Radio Scotland. I got a meeting with a producer. This is a good play, he said, but go away and write me another one. I asked if there was a problem with the subject matter. No, no, the producer assured me, you can write about anything you like. We do not have taboo subjects at the BBC. I asked if he'd like a play about the clap. No, no, you can write about anything you like except the clap. So he got a play about boxing. Four or five radio plays later, I wrote my best one. It was about blowing up Maggie Thatcher, although she wasn't, of course, called Maggie Thatcher. She wasn't even a woman in my play. The place wasn't called Scotland. And the script didn't advocate blowing up Maggie Thatcher, though if anyone needed blowing up, it was her. Suddenly, all lines of communication closed. The BBC would put on a play about anything you like as long as it isn't about blowing up the fascist regime. And it's beautifully, subtly done. It's George Orwell's best-trained dogs, the ones you don't have to show the whip to. These chaps simply understand what's taboo and what's not.

⁓⁓⁓⁓⁓⁓⁓⁓⁓

'It doesn't really matter which way you run round Arthur's Seat. Whichever way you go, you spend a lot of your time running up hill.' That's the way the first radio play started. Around then, Jerry and I could do it in about thirty minutes. That night I was so wired up I did it in twenty-eight. I was lying on the lobby carpet when Jerry came out of the living room. Mora was behind him, just leaving. She laughed when she saw the state I was in. Then she left. She was smiling and everything, perfectly composed.

After my shower, I asked Jerry how it had gone. He

said it was fine. I asked if she'd done any crying or any-thing. He said of course she hadn't. She'd be over next week sometime to use the shower again.

~~~~~~~~~~~~~~~~~

She came round a few hours before Jerry was due home from his work a week later. I made her some coffee and we sat down. Small talk lasted only a minute or so and then she started to weep again. Such tears. Such shuddering gasps. She said she was going to get him back. What could I say? I sat there feeling sorry for her, then realised I was slowly rocking back and forth, gritting my teeth. What else could I do? When she calmed down a bit, I tried to make conversation. She said she'd been learning to drive. That's good, I said. She said she was going to pass her test and then get a big white car. I asked her why the car had to be white. She said the car had to be white so she could see the blood. After she ran Doreen down in the car, she would drive home and wipe off all the blood so that no one would know it was her. She wasn't looking me in the eye when she said that. I felt my spine straighten and my head pull up and back a little as it does when something untoward and slightly threatening is beginning to happen.

~~~~~~~~~~~~~~~~~

I get violent fantasies all the time. Last night, when I couldn't get to sleep, suddenly I was in an altercation with one of the bosses at the school where I work these days. He shouted at me. I told him to be polite in that grim, flat, psycho way. He pushed me. He is a big man. Big people take a lot of hitting. They soak up blows. There's no point in having violent fantasies about tiny, crippled people. Soon this big man's face was a mask of blood. As he was going backwards, I pushed him into the window, which smashed under the weight. Then I was outside, pulling him through, over the broken, jagged edges of glass and on to the grass outside. I could go on.

Suddenly, I realised this was happening in my head and I tried to snap out of it, let it go. It's like being possessed by a series of images, taken unawares, but when you realise it's happening, you've got to let it go. Don't dwell on it.

Sexual fantasies are different. I dwell on sexual fantasies a lot, i.e., when I want to wank. I decided when I was about fourteen that sexual fantasies and wanking were perfectly okay since I found it difficult to deal with females if I didn't fantasise and masturbate. And sometimes I've turned sexual fantasies into realities, but they've never been violent, at least not since I was in the early stages of puberty. I used to fantasise about rape a lot then. I used to fantasise about raping full-grown women when I weighed about five stone and maybe therein lies the key. Maybe violent fantasies compensate for weakness. Maybe I have violent fantasies these days because I'm middle-aged and less potent than I used to be.

I don't think I had Technicolor, totally lucid, violent images popping into my head when I was going to the boxing. I was not on the surface a violent person. People I knew were very surprised that I went to the boxing. Whatever the type was, it wasn't me. I never got into trouble, arguments, or confrontations with people. Most of the time I did not look people in the eye. I was distinctly not a competitive individual. I thought people who were overtly competitive had something missing, maybe a sense of real worth or self-esteem.

But have you ever imagined being in a bar and some drunken, raj bastard starts to bear down on you with violence and madness gleaming out of his staring eyes. You will be humiliated in public by this person. This person knows violence and this is why he is bearing down on you. You do not know violence. You can dream like this in slow motion. You try to move your arms in a certain way, but you can't punch. You can't even flail. Your pride is about to be dented for ever. You're going to end up whimpering and pleading. Your self-esteem might never recover. You won't even know what it feels like to get hit.

I thought going to the boxing would help me deal with this kind of situation. First of all, I'd know how to punch, although this probably wouldn't be much use to me. If someone beat me up in a pub, I'd probably be drunk, and drunken fights usually only last for one or two blows. Afterwards I'd probably think what an asshole I was to get into this situation, but psychic damage would really be minimal.

I got to put this to the test around two in the morning when I was walking down Lothian Road a couple of years ago. The wife of a friend of mine had been round at my house and said she didn't want to walk home on her own. Fuçking hell. I was not happy with this, but agreed to walk her back to her house. I was going down the Lothian Road wearing a parka, the kind made famous by trainspotters. It was cold. The hood was up and pulled out. The snorkel-jacket effect. Someone punched me in the eye as I passed the bus stop near Princes Street. My glasses were smashed, my head banged off the railings. Fortunately, that was all that happened. The asshole who did it waltzed off. I was annoyed at myself later for being such a mark, but that was all. Lothian Road at that time of the weekend is apparently full of little wankers like that. I didn't know at the time, but I do now.

⁓⁓⁓⁓⁓⁓⁓

I did not have violent fantasies when I went to the boxing and I wasn't at all sure what to make of what Mora was saying to me about the white car and wiping off the blood. I tried to tell her that it wasn't really Doreen's fault. She said Doreen had been going out with him while he was staying with her. I said . . . I said . . . I asked her if she'd like another cup of coffee. She was in the shower again when Jerry came home from his work. When she came out of the shower, Jerry went into it. When they were both out, I went into the wee kitchen to make the dinner. While the tatties were boiling, I sat in the living room with them. Mora was smiling and happy. Jerry was managing to deal with the whole thing on a friendly level, the way mature, grown-up people are supposed to do. I didn't know how Mora managed it then. No weeping, no tears, or recriminations. Big smiles, laughing. She asked him to come and see her new flat. He agreed to visit the next weekend. I switched on the early evening news. I did not feel at all easy about the way things were developing.

⁓⁓⁓⁓⁓⁓⁓

It got worse. Jerry had arranged to go around to her flat late on the Saturday afternoon. On the Friday night the usual amount of drunkenness and drug abuse went down and the living room was a complete shambles the next day. Lemonade bottles with dregs of home brew lay on their sides around the floor. Ashtrays were brimming.

Plates with half-eaten things on them balanced on the edge of chairs. I saw it all after I opened the door and let Poisonous in. He didn't comment on the long army surplus shirt I was wearing as a nightgown or the woolly socks I had on. I showed him into the living room with my eyes still half closed and he gave me a look before saying, 'Huh.' Poisonous didn't have to say anything else. 'Huh' said it all.

Jerry was sitting amid the squalor in his white teeshirt and bare feet. He had an album cover on his knee and was rolling a stick.

'Fuck sake, Jerry,' I said. I felt awful. I had the usual Saturday morning hangover mingling with the onset of flu. 'The landlord said he was comin' today.'

'No sweat, man,' said Jerry airily. 'Take ten minutes to tidy the place up.'

Poisonous sat down, looking even neater than usual among the debris.

'Ah'll have tae stay in bed the day,' I said.

Before retiring I asked Jerry to tidy up and fold up his bed. I was feeling pretty bad. I did not want to speak to the landlord. We'd been lucky with the landlord up till then. He usually came through the week and during working hours. He always dropped me a line saying when. He used to ask after my wife. He'd never seen my wife because my wife did not exist. My job did not exist either and he must have sussed that much out rather quickly. I don't know why he'd decided to come round on a Saturday. I suspected that he was hoping to catch sight of my wife, but I suspected that the day before and the next day, what with the hangover and the flu, it had gone out of my mind. I told Jerry to tell him I was sick, hold him at the door and pay the rent from the rent tin in the kitchen. I went back to bed.

I'd been lying there for all of two minutes when the

doorbell went. I did not hear much of what was said. Jerry left the landlord at the door and went away for the rent. The wee bastard just walked into the flat then and stood looking through the living-room door.

'Oh, my God,' was apparently what he said. He told Jerry he wanted to see me. Right away.

'Right away?' said Jerry.

'Right away,' said the wee bastard grimly.

'Right away, eh?' said Jerry.

'Right away,' said the wee bastard.

'Right away, eh?' said Jerry with a wee laugh.

The trouble with Jerry was that he did not know how to look servile and he did not know how to grovel to landlords. The most they ever got out of Jerry was a shrug of the shoulders. This was because Jerry was secretly a rich-bastard-in-waiting and not just a lorry driver. Jerry came from a wee village in Ayrshire where they used to dig coal and make steel. Now, of course, after getting Maggied, they just take drugs and drink themselves to death. But Jerry's father, although he was loath to leave his council house and his pals, had set up a thriving engineering business in Paisley. Jerry's father had sent him to Edinburgh University to become an engineer, but Jerry wanted nothing to do with any of that at the time. He wanted to be a hippy and drive lorries. I used to wonder if the fact that he was going to inherit some money made Jerry as relaxed about things as he was, but Jerry just didn't give a fuck anyway.

So I'm standing there in my army shirt and woolly socks trying to be servile and grovel to the dwarf landlord. It wasn't working. He asked where my wife was. I just looked at him. I'd forgotten I was supposed to have a wife.

'And who is that person, that person in the teeshirt and the bare feet?' he spluttered.

He said he wanted me out of the flat. Start looking now. I had a couple of months. A couple of months, ken? But start looking now. I crushed the fivers into his hand and showed him the door. I knew it wasn't going to be one of my better days when I got up that morning.

chapter five

The worst kind of landlords are the kind who only own one flat. They want to make a few bob out of it without paying any tax, and they want you to walk around their flat wearing rubber gloves, dressed from head to toe in clingfilm so that you can never leave a mark on their furniture. This is despite the fact that their furniture is a pile of shite you could buy out a second-hand shop for fourpence. I have an enduring hatred of these aspiring, petty bourgeois little bastards. I was staying in a place without a lease, without getting any receipts, cash on the nail every month, and this little bastard wanted me out because he didn't like parties. This did not stop me bawling at Jerry immediately after showing the wee shite out the flat.

Jerry was a very hard person to have an argument with. Jerry was not the arguing type. You could see he wasn't good at raising his voice. Shouting was altogether foreign to him. I could shout, but not very well. I would feel like killing people before it came anywhere near shouting. But I gave a reasonable impression that day. I told Jerry he'd have to get out. I told Jerry it was impossible to pretend to be a married couple with him living in the flat. He and I did not look like a married couple. Even a squint-eyed, myopic Martian could see that we weren't a married couple. Jerry said he'd nowhere to go. I said he had a job. He could go anywhere he liked. I said I didn't have a job. If I didn't have a job, I couldn't raise the deposit for a new flat, etc., etc. Jerry said I couldn't evict him just because some bastard was trying to evict me. He was right, of course. I had to say I was sorry. We'd string the wee shite along for a couple of months, keep the place tidy, and hope he'd forget about Jerry. What the landlord made of Poisonous I don't know. Poisonous was so incongruous sitting there that the landlord probably didn't even see him.

I only ever had one other argument with Jerry. It was over the last grass plant. I was guarding the last grass plant in the hope that it would flower, but deferred gratification wasn't Jerry's strong suit. There was only him and his brother in the family and he was far younger. His mother must have stuffed his face with sweeties. Jerry was a consumer. Jerry did not have an ascetic bone in his body, but Jerry wasn't altogether a greedy bastard. Jerry wanted to share things. Jerry would half things with you, but he always got the big half. When we had no money and no dope, Jerry wanted to smoke the last plant. I told him it was mine. Fatal mistake. He chopped it down. I was apoplectic with rage. I couldn't believe he'd chopped it down. He said it was ready to come down and he knew it was ready because he had an O Level in biology. There's no way you can argue against that kind of logic. I could have hit him, but we hit each other a couple of times a week as it was, so hitting him would have been silly.

I used some of the stuff that happened between me and
Jerry in the play about the nurse getting busted and losing
his job. Funnily enough, the play was called *Busted*. The
nurse in the play also got chucked out of his flat, an
event brought about by the arrival of a somewhat anarchic
flatmate, a person quite unlike Jerry. It wasn't a great
drama, but it was funny. People would burst out laughing
reading the script. I thought I'd try to get it put on after
my first radio play was so well received. I got a list of all
the theatre companies in Scotland and sent every one of
them a letter, describing the play and asking if they'd like
to read it. No one replied. Without asking them to read
it, I sent a copy to the Traverse, a theatre which was
supposed to exist for new drama. I got it back so long
after sending it to them that I'd forgotten they had it. So
if anyone is reading this who has a wonderful play and
fondly imagines that just because it's wonderful someone
is bound to want to do it, think again. Theatre companies
exist for the amusement and profit of the people who run
them and that's not you, baby.

Boxing shows are a kind of theatre and much better drama
than anything. In really good fights, right up until the last
bell you don't know how it's going to end. Even after the
fight's finished, you sometimes don't know who's won and
who's lost. The actors aren't pretending either. Sometimes
you see people involved in desperate situations. Sometimes people are leaking blood, teetering on the edge of
exhaustion and unconsciousness. Sometimes you see
people who are suddenly plain unconscious and then it's

like winter when you're not sure if there's ever going to be a spring. Boxing is really scary.

I always felt a nervousness when I went down to Meadow-bank Stadium to train. I used to think, 'This is crazy.' Even if I didn't feel particularly nervous going into the stadium, my guts always tightened up when I put on the sixteen-ounce gloves. After sparring and hitting the bags or whatever, I always felt wonderful. I felt clean somehow. And I was coming along. One night after training, just as I was about to go for a shower, Wee Benny and Bill the Trainer took me into a wee room at the other side of the corridor. They put me on the scales. I was stripped to the waist and wearing just shorts. I'd never been looked up and down like that before. Two men were blatantly checking out my body. I felt very odd standing on the scales. It was like being meat. They looked at me the way surgeons are supposed to, without passion.

'Sixty-eight kilos,' said Bill.

'He'll sweat a bit of that off yet,' said Wee Benny.

'Whit's sixty-eight kilos?' I asked.

'Welterweight,' said Wee Benny. 'You're a kilo over ten an' a half stone. Whit height are ye, son?'

'Five foot ten in ma stockin' soles,' I said.

In three months I'd lost a stone in weight. I was up to training practically every day. On the days when we didn't go to the boxing, Jerry and I would run round Arthur's Seat. I'd even run round Arthur's Seat on the days after I'd been drunk. I'd wear layers of woolly jumpers and sweat it all out. The only days I definitely wouldn't train was after I'd been taking speed. The days after I'd been taking speed, I'd avoid running in case I fell down with a heart attack, but it's the drink that knocks the shit out of you. You can easily distinguish the effects of drugs if you train a lot. It's the legal ones that really fuck you up, of course, but I'd stopped smoking fags while I was still in South Clerk Street and we only had dope at the weekends. I was getting fit and kind of falling in love with myself.

Mora came round the day before Jerry was due to visit her flat. I don't know why she came round that day. Maybe it was the shower. Maybe it was because nobody else would listen to her. Maybe she'd nobody else to weep in front of. I thought it would stop, but it started again as soon as I handed her the cup of coffee. She said she wished that she could give Doreen a cup of coffee so that she could poison her. If she could ever get Doreen round to her flat, she'd feed her rat poison because rat poison was horrible stuff and it made you die really badly, in terrible agony, wriggling and writhing about while great holes were burnt in your insides. I held my breath.

'You're not goiny poison Jerry, are ye?' I asked, a little tentatively. She gave a semi-hysterical half laugh amid the tears then. No, she was going to get Jerry back. She was going to use magic on Jerry. She had a bit of one of his old shirts which she'd been using as a floor cloth. She was going to dip that in his coffee and put in some of her blood. I don't know why I didn't tell Jerry that. I could have. Somehow it was confidential. Somehow Mora put you in a position where you automatically colluded with her. I asked him afterwards how his visit had gone. Fine, he said.

'Did she give ye a cup of coffee?'

'Yeah,' he said.

'Whit kind of coffee was it?' I asked. I could feel the smile coming on.

'Coffee, man. Coffee coffee.'

'Did it taste at all of floor cloths?'

'Did it fuck, man. Whit are ye goin' on about?' I could see that I had him by then. He wanted to know whatever it was.

'Did it taste of blood an' floor cloths by any chance?'

'It tasted of coffee. As in coffee an' milk an' sugar.'

'Not coffee as in coffee, milk, sugar, blood an' floor cloths?'

'Get tae fuck! Whit are ye goin' on about?'

'Ah'm not at liberty tae divulge ma sources, Jerry, but the next time ye go there, Ah wouldn't eat or drink anythin' if Ah was you. She's started castin' spells, man. Abramelon the Mage hasn't a fuckin' look-in. Was she always mad?'

'Yeah.'

'Naw, she wisny.'

⁓⁓⁓⁓⁓⁓⁓⁓

About nine years after I wrote *Busted*, I was a housewife. It was wonderful being a housewife at first because I didn't have to go to work and I had some money. But it's also a wee bit boring being a housewife. I thought I'd see if I had any credibility with anyone then, since I'd already had about three or four radio plays done and one of my books had been published. If I got *Busted* on, I thought life might not be so one-paced. I wrote letters to everyone again about *Busted* and again got no replies. Then I contacted the Gateway Exchange. This was set up by Jimmy Boyle and his wife, Sarah, to help rehabilitate criminals and junkies and people like that. I'd met Jimmy Boyle when he was in the Special Unit in Barlinnie Prison because one of my brothers used to lock him up.

You don't half meet a bunch of wankers when you hang

about in drama. Usually, the only people who are worth a shit are the actors and technicians. Nearly everyone else I met went around worrying about their so-called careers, and they backbit about each other, and bitched all the time. There's just a little cake and as more and more people try to get on it, more and more people try to push them off. But it wasn't like that when I went down to see Jimmy Boyle at the Gateway Exchange. We were all Jock Tamson's bairns down there. The guy who was running the theatre for him read the script and said they'd do it. Not only would they do it, they'd tour it. Five actors and a lights man in an old Post Office van went all over the place. It's called profit-share. I forwent my profits and I don't suppose anyone else got paid enough to buy a bag of chips. It was wonderful. The Triangle Club in Pilton. My short life in the theatre started there.

A couple of years later I'm going down Shaftesbury Avenue in London. There's all these theatres. Writers are on ten per cent of the bums on seats. Half the writers seem to be with this agent I'm going to see. This is big bucks. I'm on my way to see the man who's taken over the Margaret Ramsay Agency, a Mr Tom Erhardt.

I should have known it was never going to work out when I got the first phone call from him. I'd re-written the play for someone who wanted it do it on the Fringe. The production was miscast, but the play was brilliant by this time. I thought so, anyway. I sent it to the Margaret Ramsay Agency because I saw a movie about Joe Orton. Unfortunately, Margaret Ramsay was dead by the time I wrote to her, but Tom Erhardt wasn't. I was in the middle of making the dinner when I got the call. The tatties are boiling, the kid's greetin', I hadn't had a fag for three days, the works. A North American accent asks to speak to me.

'Graham, if ye don't stop speakin' in that fuckin' stupid accent, Ah'm goiny put down the fuckin' phone. Awright?' I said.

A month or two later I'm going down Shaftesbury Avenue looking for St Martin's Lane. I can't find it. It starts to drizzle. I went into a pub and asked the barman. The alley I was looking for was practically next door. I phoned up and asked if the man was in. I was told he finished lunch at two. He wasn't in at two. I had a pint. I phoned again. I had another pint. I phoned again. I had another pint. I phoned again. I had another pint. I phoned again. Fuck this, thinks I. I'll go up and talk to the secretary. Before doing this, I went down to the bogs and rolled myself a joint. I allowed myself to smoke joints then, though I didn't allow myself to smoke fags. I was half pissed and gasping for nicotine.

I'm standing outside the entryphone at the exact address. It's in an alley. A picturesque alley, but an alley none the less. I've just lit up the stick when a policeman appears at the bottom of the alley. I cannot believe this. He's wearing a cape and everything. Evenin' all. How would you like to bring your exotic cigarette down to the station with me, sir? I ring the doorbell. Beam me up. I blunder into the office at the top of the stairs. The secretary's cool and offers me a coffee. I sit on the floor and do in the stick. I ask her the three questions I want to ask and then decide it's time to go. But I reckon I could roll a stick to smoke as I walk along Shaftesbury Avenue again. I turn my back not quite discreetly on the secretary and roll it on top of the filing cabinet. I'm just about to leave when Tom Erhardt comes bounding up the stairs.

I'd never seen a man having a harder time than this man behind the desk. He's rubbing his face. He's pushing

whatever hair he's got left about the top of his head while
the dope smoke billows around the room. Some of us
maybe do better staying home behind the keyboards.

Meetings with Mora were still hard graft. The pattern
seemed well established after three or four visits. She'd
ring the doorbell and I'd stop writing. I'd give her coffee.
She'd weep. She'd tell me insane things that worried me
a bit. I assured myself that it was all in her head, that
she'd get over this Jerry business and everyone would live
happily ever after in the end. Somehow, she managed to
transform herself in the shower. She always seemed happy
enough after that. A little later Jerry would come in from
his work and Mora would be much as I remembered her
when I stayed with them in Marchmont. She was wonderful when she laughed. Her whole spirit beamed. Not
that it was doing her any good with Jerry. He was being
nice in a kind of offhand way.

'Ah'd much rather sleep with Doreen,' he said one night
when we were on our own and drinking beer.

'Whit's the difference?'

'She was really inhibited.'

'Mora?' I said, surprised. 'Fuck sake, Jerry, if ye sleep
with someone fur six months without screwin' them,
they're bound tae seem a bit inhibited.'

'Naw, before that,' he said.

Jerry and I weren't liable to talk about sex except in the
most general kind of way, so I didn't pursue what he
meant by inhibited. But we both knew the people Mora
had stayed with before Jerry and Poisonous moved in on
her. One of them told me Mora had had kennels full of
boyfriends before she started with Jerry. Virgins you
expect to be inhibited, or just plain ignorant. Somehow

you don't expect women who sleep with lots of men to be inhibited. Anyway, I didn't feel any more comfortable than Jerry when talking about the sexual behaviour of women we knew, not unless I was drunk as a skunk or speeding out of my head of course.

Then one day Mora appeared at the flat and seemed completely different. She said she'd decided to start having a good time. She'd heard of a dance where a big band would be playing. It was kind of gala night with sword-swallowers, ballet dancers, that kind of stuff. Of course, she wanted me to come along. I felt a slight twinge of uneasiness about this, but I tried to dismiss it. She wasn't going there to get off with me. That didn't seem a realistic possibility. But I was concerned enough to ask who else she wanted to come along. She said she'd asked the Assistant Head and his wife.

The Assistant Head and his wife had both gone to the same high school in Stirling as Mora. I'd known them both all the time I was at Edinburgh University. Before he left university, the Assistant Head had cut his hair and smartened up his appearance. Then he'd gone to Moray House to train as a teacher. When he wasn't teaching, he spent most of the time stoned. The Assistant Head was like a great many of the people in my generation. They don their armour and Dr Jekyll it to work. Back in their homes, they Mr Hyde it. Being the children of the usual middle-class parents, they spent all their young adult years pretending to their mums and dads that they didn't take illegal drugs. Now they pretend to their children that they're the usual middle-class parents. In their professional capacities, they sometimes go around telling adolescents just to say no, except in the case of the Assistant Head. He tells them not to get caught.

Mora said some other people were supposed to be coming with us, but they didn't show up at the pub in Stockbridge. Unlike most Scottish people who are, in fact, mean bastards, the Assistant Head always poured lots of drinks down my throat when he saw me. I didn't care by the time he said he and his wife weren't going to go to the dance hall. Me and Mora left them on the pavement across the road from Tiffany's, the dance hall, and he said later that we seemed determined to have a good time. We waltzed across the road. We paid the man at the door and got a small table to ourselves at the edge of the dance floor. The music was very loud. I leant over and shouted in her ear and she couldn't hear me, so I grabbed hold of her and pulled her on to my knee.

Around that time I didn't go to the boxing for a while. You could go to the club three times a week if you wanted to, but one of these sessions was on Sunday afternoon and Jerry and I never made it to that one. We usually went on Tuesdays and Thursdays, but if you happened to miss a week and went back, you always got a sore nose. Someone would always punch you bang on the nose. When I went regularly, that never happened to me. I was into the noble art of self-defence and nobody wore headguards. My main priority was to avoid being hit. I wasn't there to win anything. I didn't like getting punched on the nose particularly, but I always got punched on the nose when my timing and balance were a bit off.

A couple of sparring sessions and I was back to being as good as I'd ever been, which was not very good. But I could be relatively relaxed in the sparring and nobody seemed to want to kill me, anyway. I must have seemed a bit strange to them, being nearly ten years older than most of them and having the long hair. But I was still coming along.

One night, just after Bill the Trainer had let me out of the ring, Wee Benny was waiting to speak to me.

'You're gettin' a lot fitter, son,' he said. I told him about me and Jerry running round Arthur's Seat. He shouted for Bill the Trainer to come over and speak to him a minute.

'Do ye think he's ready fur a contest, Bill?' said Wee Benny.

Bill the Trainer must have been involved in chainsaw massacres in his youth. It was as if he'd come through a massive amount of turbulence somewhere which had left him with a deep, quiet centre. He was not fazed by anything. He didn't say much, but if he said something, you listened. I was all ears when Wee Benny asked him that. I was suddenly aware of my whole body. Nobody had mentioned anything about contests to me before. I'd never asked for any.

'He looks fit enough,' said Bill the Trainer. Wee Benny told him I'd been running round Arthur's Seat. 'Three two-minute rounds won't be any bother then. You'll dae awright, son.'

Bill the Trainer got back into the ring then and Wee Benny started telling me he'd get me a novice just like myself, someone who'd never boxed before. He said there was a show coming off in three weeks' time. I hadn't said much. Suddenly, Wee Benny stopped talking and looked at me.

'Do you want a contest, son?' he asked.

'Yes,' I said.

chapter six

~~~~~~~~~~~~

While the band thumped on, and the ballet dancers twirled, and the fire-eaters blew out flames, Mora and I behaved rather badly. Teenagers in a public place would have been told to pack it in. I rubbed my hands all over her, everywhere. There didn't seem to be much of a reason to hold back at first because Mora was flatter-chested than me. What are you supposed to say to someone who's groping something you haven't come equipped with? Mora didn't say anything. I shouted in her ear, but she still couldn't hear me very well, even sitting on my knee. We clung to each other on the dance floor. I spent all the money I had on booze. That didn't take long. After sobering up a bit, we could have left it at that. But she said she had enough dope in her flat for two sticks.

I stubbed out the last one and didn't really know what I was supposed to do after that. I was sitting at the foot of a pine bed. Mora came down the bed and put her arms round my neck. I don't know why. I could have gone home, but when she put her arms round my neck, I assumed I was supposed to fuck her instead.

I hauled her up to the top of the bed and pulled off her shiny red velvet trousers. I found this very unreal. I started fiddling around with her. Her flesh seemed dead and pallid. Her head leant over to the side and she looked away.

I don't know what she was thinking, but it looked like another human sacrifice.

~~~~~~~~~~~~~~~~~~~~~~~~~~~~~~~~~~

I don't know why people bother, if they're going to act like that. You'd have more fun humping a tailor's dummy. Maybe it's embarrassment. Maybe they look away and lie still because they're shy. Maybe they think it's expected of them to lie there and give you something while pretending to be dead. Just makes me want to shake some life into them. But why do they bother? It must be some kind of deal they think will secure them an advantage of some sort. Maybe they think men won't stick with them if they seem to enjoy it.

~~~~~~~~~~~~~~~~~~~~~~~~~~~~~~~~~~

She was wearing a very nice, short, silky smock. It is slightly obscene getting balled with half your clothes still on, but it does allow one the opportunity to ball someone with all their clothes off afterwards. I felt ever so slightly annoyed after screwing Mora the first time. I hadn't asked at any time if she was on the pill. I assumed, being of that generation and knowing her past, that she would be. But I was aware of not asking. I wanted her to say something if she wasn't. She didn't say anything, so I pulled the rest of her clothes off and balled her again. She seemed slightly more alive that time. I had the feeling that the more I worked on her, the more responsive she'd get.

~~~~~~~~~~~~~~~~~~~~~~~~~~~~~~~~~~

Wee Benny used to talk about getting broken up. He used to tell people in the gym who arrived late and wanted to spar to go and get broken up. It means you sweat and pant, maybe enough for the natural morphines to check in, and then you're broken up. You're flexible, relaxed, sweating and ready to go to work.

After the second time, she put out the light and I took off my clothes. We went under the covers. I felt comfortable in the dark and she, for the first time, felt warm. Her hole was sopping and easy enough to intrude upon. She was broken up. She was with me that time. In my ear, gasping and panting. Then I fell into a kind of half sleep. Languorously, at some point, I rolled over her and balled her again. I knew it was there. I didn't have to ask for it. It wasn't a meal at set times. It was a buffet and you could have it when you wanted it.

I wakened up with her sucking on my cock. I must say I was a bit surprised. She must have started sucking it when it was flaccid because it was only half hard when I wakened up. It hadn't been stiff long before she climbed on to it. She hung her head so I couldn't see her face. She shuttled back and forth. It was great just to lie there and not have to do anything. She gave an 'Uh' and dropped her head into the crook of my neck. I left her there a little bit and then rolled her over and balled her again.

The sex got better the more we did it, but we didn't talk about sex at all. No one mentioned riding, or fucking, or shagging, or even screwing. We didn't mention it at all.

She just asked me not to tell Jerry. I didn't know why this
was. I asked her if she was sure. She seemed very sure. I
didn't think I needed to ask her why. I assumed it was
because she still wanted Jerry back and if I told him about
me sleeping with her, well ... I agreed quite readily to
this since I didn't want to go through the hassle of telling
Jerry right then. But I knew Jerry would be as all right as
you could be about your pal screwing your ex-girlfriend.
Jerry was not a jealous guy. And right then, I was feeling
pretty good about the whole thing. I really liked Mora
anyway, but that morning I liked her even more.

She had a phone. I asked if I could phone and come
round sometime. She was sitting on my thighs in tight,
tight trousers. I was rubbing my hand along between her
legs. She said sure.

I spent the rest of the day and evening in a terrific
mood. I told Jerry I'd met someone I used to sleep with
occasionally when I lived in South Clerk Street. Jerry
didn't mind who I slept with. I knew that. I wanted to tell
him I was lying, that I'd been sleeping with Mora, but I
didn't. I assumed I'd have to tell him sometime. I didn't
want to tell him right then. He knew we had gone to
Tiffany's, but he couldn't imagine me sleeping with Mora
either.

I went down the corridor towards the showers feeling
completely exhilarated after Wee Benny told me about
the fight he was going to arrange for me. I was going to
fight someone. Me. Little old me. In a boxing ring, going
biff biff in front of lots of people. It was too crazy to be

true. At best it was absurd. I was the Marijuana Kid. My
hair was way down my back. I had to put it into tons of
elastic bands just to spar. I'd never hit anyone in anger
since I was a kid. I was in my mid-twenties, an honours
graduate with no job and no prospects. But I could throw
a straight left and a straight right. That was all. I hadn't
ever thrown a hook or an uppercut. By the time I reached
the showers that little worm of worry had begun to gnaw.
Brain damage. Brutalisation. A burst nose. Black eyes. A
very sore face. A total humiliation. Round one. Ding ding.
Bang and you're out. It happens. The little worm was
always there. You just knew it was better not to examine
it too closely.

The violence in a boxing club is something you can volunteer for any time you like. Maybe that's why I don't
remember having violent fantasies then. You don't want
to dwell on the consequences, on the blood and snotter
aspects of it. I used to fantasise about winning things like
world titles, Olympic titles, British titles. It was easier to
fantasise about that than winning Eastern Districts titles
because I'd never seen anyone winning one of those.
Winning a world title might be a fantasy that would pop
into my head when I was running round Arthur's Seat,
but I even stopped imagining things like that when I got
told I was going to have a fight.

A fight. I was going to have a fight. I went around
telling people this and trying to believe it myself. I was in
a guy's flat a night or two later doing a line of speed.
Immediately after snorting it, I started telling him why
I'd have to stop doing things like that. I had a fight to
fight. The boy couldn't believe it. I said it was going to be
a novice just like myself. We'd both be terrified. We'd

be shaking like leaves in this strange, strange situation. But it was unlikely that my opponent would have done as much acid as I had and he, therefore, would not be as familiar with weird situations and mental states as I was. I had taken lots of different kinds of drugs in my time so the boy wouldn't stand a chance.

I wasn't sure what I was supposed to do. Stop taking drugs. Well, take as many drugs as people will give you for free because that won't amount to much. But leave off the speed. Don't take speed. It was harder to imagine not drinking. Jerry had stayed off the drink for three weeks when he had the clap and that seemed a truly heroic effort. I wouldn't have a drink for a week or so beforehand. Then there was the sex. That was a bit of a problem. There probably wasn't a rule about sex as such. Orgasms is what they're talking about. Spunk. Keep your spunk. Turn into a spunky kind of a guy. The longest I'd gone without an orgasm since I was a youth was probably three days. After three days my goolies were aching. Not having sex for three weeks was easily imagined, but not having a wank for a week seemed impossible.

An ex-professional boxer told me once that he'd managed not to have an orgasm for two weeks once. He came when his girlfriend unzipped him afterwards. We're born to sin.

I started to masturbate thinking about Mora. I'd run it through my head, and re-run it, and run it again. Nothing changed. I imagined it just the way it was and always would be. I wasn't imagining doing something to her which I hadn't done. What we'd done was so unexpected. In itself it was enough. When it wasn't enough, I went out and phoned her.

The phone box was a five-minute walk away, across the London Road and up a bit. I felt excited just walking into it. Can I come round? She said yes. I used to think, 'I'm going to phone up and see if I can get some sex tonight.' Usually, I used the phone to see if I could score. Can I come round? It used to be the same question. Sometimes they said no, but she said yes.

I was sitting in her living room, drinking coffee. There was nothing much to say. I started feeling a bit anxious and nervous after a few minutes of this. I was waggling my toes and clenching my teeth a little. You don't know if it's going to happen, or how it's going to happen, or how to start it happening. When a natural lull occurred in the conversation, I couldn't keep still any longer. I pulled her on to the floor and started taking her knickers and tights off. I couldn't talk to her. She started unzipping my jeans and pulling them down. She was giggling. I mounted her as quickly as I could and we did it on the floor. It was a kind of assertion on my part. I couldn't stand the doubt of wondering if it might not happen. Right after that, we took off all our clothes and went to bed.

It happened like that a couple of times. I could easily have fallen in love then. She was so giving and loving. Doreen had said the same about Jerry the day after she'd first slept with him. I could imagine Mora and Jerry together quite easily. The lazy intertwinings. All it would have taken was a bit of conversation, the way you do to find out about people, what they've been up to, who with, and whether they're the kind of person you'd want to fall in love with. But if we'd talked, we'd have had to talk about Jerry. I didn't want to ask her about anything like that in case some madness came out. When I was able to forget about that, Mora was just the kind of person you'd want to hug. I could have fallen in love with her, but I decided I wasn't going to. She wanted Jerry. She'd said so. My girlfriend was in Australia, but that's not like being dead or divorced. Mora had me then, but only for the present, when I was there. And I loved being there. She had very flexible shoulders and would put her arm round my neck while I lay on her big pine bed. Sometimes it felt wonderful.

She sucked my cock a lot, as if it was no big deal. She made it seem like a natural part of the business. I was surprised by this since I'd been told she was inhibited. Maybe he didn't mean that. Maybe Mora had decided to behave differently from now on in. It was hard to tell, especially if you didn't want to ask. You assume if someone's been to bed with lots of people that they've been round the course and back again in tackety boots. This might not be the case. Maybe they've been to bed with lots of people because they can't keep just one and not because they like different stokes. Maybe when they're going to bed with all kinds of different people, all they're doing is opening their legs and looking off into the middle distance somewhere.

One infers what one can. She was hopeless at wanking. I assumed this was because she hadn't spent the initial years of her adolescence jerking people off. She'd probably given in immediately or maybe didn't have boyfriends till she'd decided to go the whole hog. Anyway, she was crap at that. This made her blowjobs a more lingering experience, less a way of getting the business done.

Getting the business done became a top priority when there was only a couple of weeks to go before the fight. I started to train every day. I'd been running three or four times a week, but now I ran in the morning and trained on the nights when I wasn't at the club. Jerry brought home 'Never Mind the Bollocks'. Never was there a better album to skip and jump about to. Jerry would put it on loud and I'd start skipping in the hall. After a bit, Jerry would time me for two minutes of shadow boxing. Then I'd do press-ups, squats and sit-ups for a minute. Then I'd do two minutes' shadow boxing. Then I'd do the press-ups and all that. Then I'd go back to the shadow boxing and finish up with the circuits of press-ups, et cetera. After that, I'd lie on the floor feeling totally trashed. I started going round in a kind of fuzzy, irritated daze. I was sparring like someone in a trance. Wee Benny told me to pack it in. I was training too hard, but nothing concentrates the mind like a date with some ritualised violence. It creeps closer. It preys on you. Sometimes it'll make you seem serious and preoccupied. It's like being in trouble with the law. You can't get it out of your mind. Like a money worry or worrying about having somewhere to stay.

The landlord was being a pain. Funnily enough, the flat was far tidier with Jerry staying there than it had been with me on my own. I didn't leave my dirty clothes sitting in the sink for days at a stretch. We washed the dishes every couple of days. His foam-filled sofa bed was becoming a bit of a fetid swamp in the corner of the living room, but even that looked all right on the odd occasions when Jerry could be bothered folding it up. But the dwarf started showing up at the door at odd times and asking about adverts from me which he hadn't seen in the newspapers. I'd get ratty with Jerry sometimes. The implementation of strong-arm tactics was mentioned by the dwarf one day. One guy we knew had just been thrown into the street. The polis said it was a civil matter. Jerry and I agreed if we killed the first person over the doorstep we'd probably keep the tenancy a bit longer. It cannot be a civil matter when you've used a baseball bat to brain someone who's just kicked your door in. Then Jerry kicked in the door himself when he forgot his keys one day. It didn't help the sense of impermanence. Even when we cleaned up the place specially for the next rent day. I told Jerry the problem was him sitting there. He said he could hide. You've got to laugh. I said, 'Where?' He said, 'In the bedroom cupboard.' The doorbell rang. Jerry actually got into the bedroom cupboard. It was Poisonous. I pretended he was the landlord and walked him slowly into the bedroom where I stood outside the cupboard explaining the problems I had living with Jerry, how he was mentally defective and how I'd promised my uncle I'd look after him. There's nothing as withering as the look from Poisonous when he finds you shrunk into the corner of a cupboard, balanced precariously on top of a toolbox, with a look of horror etched on your face as the light of day cuts across it. It was time to start thinking seriously about doing a moonlight. But in the meantime there was a bit more money going around since I stopped paying the bills when the wee rat turned nasty.

It was stupid. I didn't have any great feelings of hate for that landlord. I didn't fantasise about throwing him down the stairs or anything. I thought he had an unfortunate attitude. I did not regard him as an opponent.

I did not even regard my opponent as being an opponent. I did not imagine pummelling him till streams of blood were squishing from wounds on his face, or battering him into insensibility. I didn't know what kind of attitude I should have, since I'd never fought before. I couldn't feel any animosity towards him. I didn't know him. I didn't even know what he looked like. I was told he'd be a novice just like me. Just like me. He'd be just like me. I wondered if I should regard him as some kind of mad brute, a crazy psychopath who wanted to batter me about and knock holy fuck out of me without knowing what a nice person I really was. And not the kind of chap who was cut out for this rough stuff. Or should I think how miraculous the human body was and have every respect for the wonderment who was going to try and beat the crap out of me? I had to settle for thinking whoever it was was a brave bastard for getting into a boxing ring in the first place. Brave and mad, maybe a mixture of both. I tried to concentrate on where he'd be. I was trying to develop a good sense of where my fists stopped. That's where his head would have to be. A nice impersonal round target, full of blood and spit and mucus, which you can hit as hard as you like.

I tried to explain the target area in boxing to some kids once. There is the jawline at the point of the chin and stretching up a little on either side. There is the point just below and between where the ribs join under the breast-bone. Everything else, I said, was a miss. If you get hit round the jaw there, or on the solar plexus, you will fall down. There is nothing you can do to stop yourself falling down. Down you'll go, whether you want to or not. The aim of boxing is to stop the other guy hitting you and the best way to do that is to make him fall down.

Somebody won't fall down if you hit him on the eye. A blow on the eye will probably make you blind for a second or two, your eye might water, you might get cut, but you won't fall down. Ditto with a punch on the nose. Of course, if Mike Tyson hit you on the elbow, he'd knock you down, but we're talking here nearer the normal scale. I don't know why taking a punch on the jaw near the chin makes you fall down, but when someone collapses due to a punch on the head, it's a frightening thing.

The bell goes and I'm standing out there. I'm as nervous as hell. Me and the boy start flailing at each other. We're missing, scuffling. There's something wrong. I can feel that there's something wrong, but I'm not sure what it is. I talk to myself. This is a fatal error, showing lack of concentration. Just steady up, I said. Start catching him with your left. The next thing I heard was four! I was on my hands and knees. The referee was waving his finger at me. Four! I do not know what happened between nothing and four. Nothing happened after the fern-like red flash went up the side of my head. Four, the man said.

It was like being dead. There was nothing till four. It could have been five million, four hundred thousand and twenty-four. There was no time there. It was just a gap. I knew to stay down till eight. Get up at eight. The referee is staring into my face. I know he'll be checking my eyes to see if the pupils are the same size, or if one is birling in one direction while the other lolls about at the bottom of its socket. So I lean forward and open my eyes to give him a better look. I must have looked crazy doing that. And you're out!

I was walking up the stairs to the dressing room later and trying to work out what I knew and what I didn't. This is check your amnesia time. I couldn't remember my address. I could remember my name. Between my ears seemed quite empty, somehow.

The fight might have lasted half a minute, if that. I knew there was something odd about it, but it only came to me when I was walking up the stairs later. The boy was a southpaw. It was a southpaw right hook. That's cheating! Everybody knows that southpaws stand the wrong way round. And they hit you with weird punches, from directions that you don't expect. Nobody told me my opponent was a southpaw. Maybe they did not wish to worry me.

Wee Benny told me later that they would not have stopped that fight in Glasgow. I don't know what has to happen to you in Glasgow for the fight to be stopped. Your lower jaw must be sitting in the second row. Still, it doesn't do to be overmatched. You can get murdered if you're overmatched. Your man has to get you someone you can fight. But if you're told the boy you're going to be fighting is a complete novice, you should try to believe it, though it may not be true.

George the Trainer, who had never done any boxing before, was a terrible matchmaker. I never thought about who my opponent was, which made us a perfect combination. One dark winter's night we arrived at a miners' club in Shotts. George the Trainer went to speak to the organisers while I hung around. The first I saw of my opponent was when the fight was just about to start. The week before he'd fought at light heavy. He looked like my big brother. He was a huge, big person. 'Whit kind of fuckin' welterweight is that supposed tae be?' I asked the trainer just before the gumshield went in.

The guy might have arranged for me to fight someone who never showed up. Opponents sometimes get sick. Maybe he got told the boy was a welterweight and showed up to find that he'd been tucking into his porridge and had suddenly grown up to be a big boy. Maybe he got told there was a show coming up and why not bring along a couple of fighters? But when he's there and you're there, he might not get any expenses money unless you get into the ring. And the man who's organising the show has a certain number of slots to fill. That's his problem. If he's advertised ten fights, he wants ten fights. If your corner will let you fight Vlad the Impaler that's okay by him.

You didn't expect me to give you the real fight, the big fight, there, did you? You won't get that till nearer the end. But you can't be all that far from the end now. I could just jam it in right now, but then the book would be finished and it's too short to be a book yet. I'll just have to write a lot more sex. That's what I'm interested in, anyway. I've never written such a dirty book. So keep going. It gets really dirty in the next chapter.

chapter seven

~~~~~~~~~~

The trouble if you fight all the time is that you get too blasé. You can't be expected to shake and tremble every time you go into a boxing ring. But if you're a grown-up person, you're liable to be in a bit of a state the first time you do it. Nobody worries about kids. Kids get hustled into doing it whether they like it or not. No one cares about how worried the kid is as long as he does it. Jim the Welterweight once told me the worst injuries he'd received all came when he was fighting as a kid. No gumshields. A ragged, torn mouth. Try sucking a lollipop with a face like that. After fighting as a kid, nothing fazed him. He'd get stripped to box the way other people get stripped to play badminton. But if you're a grown-up, how could you forget the first time?

~~~~~~~~~~

After sleeping with Mora over a night or two, I realised she didn't want to do it backwards. Even sideways. Not even sideways before rolling over on to her belly, before going on to her hands and knees. I didn't understand this. She'd kind of slip and slide away without saying anything, without looking at you. I wondered if she thought I was going to bugger her, but I didn't believe that somehow.

Then I thought she didn't want to do it with me. I was persistent without being too persistent. I didn't believe it was a prohibition she could keep, or would want to.

So there's this old Italian novelist on the TV. He's really the usual novelist with the usual childhood spent in bed with the asthma and all that. But he's talking about sex. Sex and existentialism. He said sex was a way of connecting with other people. This did not knock me off the seat. Then he said doing it backwards has overtones, though not always necessarily, he said, of sado-masochism. I stared at the TV when he said that. There was a still of the back of a woman in a suspender belt looking away and over a balcony. Sado-masochism. I didn't get it. Then I did. You have to kind of squint.

Dog-fucking has a touch of submission and domination about it for sure. Of course, as the Italian novelist would say, this is not always necessarily the case. I wondered if this was what Mora was bothered about. Pictures of monkeys on TV banging each other, for just a little bit, just to show who's boss. I didn't know. Maybe she thought oral sex and the missionary position were enough for anyone to be going on with. Maybe she was embarrassed about her asshole. Her asshole being evident. If you don't talk about sex, it's quite hard to know. But I kept trying half-heartedly to tease her into it. Silly sexual positions can be a bit of a laugh, but that's not why I was silently encouraging her. I wanted something she didn't want to give me. Just because she didn't want to give it to me. And because she had a bum which was totally unsurpassable.

Mora was so small you could scoop your arms round her in all kinds of directions. She was encompassable. It was easy to have hands and fingers going at her from all directions. Maybe she was taken unawares when the fingers slipped in from behind when she was lying on her back with her legs bent. I knew I had her by the low moan. She groaned over on to her stomach. I knelt between her legs and stretched my fingers down into her. I didn't hurry up. I lifted her featherlight backwards on to her knees. I knew she was staring into the semi-darkness with her eyes wide and her mouth slack. I lovingly stroked her thighs and her beautiful bum. The palm of one hand glided over her buttocks. Then I reached over and broke her arms at the elbows so that she was resting on her forearms and knees. Her asshole seemed pitched kind of high. Her cunt was the same. She was built for this. I gazed at her in delight for a moment or two. Then I thought I'd have to do it in a way that would make her want to do it again, whenever I wanted. A thought sprang to mind unbidden.

'Ah'm going tae screw your fuckin' brains out!' I heard myself say to myself in a cold, staring kind of way. Where *do* they come from?

Maybe sometimes in life there are things you aren't ready for. I thought I was ready for the Traverse Theatre when I got a call from Wee Ben. Wee Ben must be distinguished from Wee Benny. Wee Ben looked rather like Wee Benny, except nobody had ever tried to flatten his face with a shovel and he was at least thirty years younger. Wee Ben was just the usual English person who comes to Scotland and wants to be a theatre director. Scotland is full of

English theatre directors. I can't think why this is. It must be the accent. The people who interview them probably don't sound Scottish and a nice middle-class English accent must sound pretty down home to them.

Wee Ben gave me a call because the Radio Scotland people were being nice about me, and *Busted* was touring at the time. People like the Traverse wait for you to do something, then jump in and discover you. They were going to discover me and three other Scottish writers even though I'd been discovered at least twice before. This time I was going to be discovered in a season of new Scottish plays. Five actors were going to divide the roles in four plays and learn them during a fortnight's rehearsal, and then perform them, sometimes two in the one night for two weeks.

Thank God I'm not an actor. Anything but that. There are millions of them. You can get them for nothing. They look haunted sometimes when you see them, especially the really good ones. Imagine thinking you could do Hamlet better than anyone and you can't even afford to buy a bag of chips. Then imagine being asked by the Traverse if you'd like to learn two major roles in two weeks and then perform them back to back for a fortnight. Of course, you'd be delighted. Young actors don't turn down the Traverse. Acting at the Traverse is sometimes a wonder to behold, but there's not much even the best can do when the script's crap.

Wee Ben and I didn't really get on. My new Scottish play was an old radio script I'd rehashed. I thought I'd cracked it when I re-wrote it, but I hadn't. There's a guy in a police cell with lots of flashbacks to a steelworks and this flat in South Clerk Street. It was supposed to have a slightly hallucinogenic feel to it, with a big expressionist kind of cell door for the four lesser characters to walk in and out of. Not the best idea I've ever had, but I thought it had a chance until I saw the model of the set. No door. Not a big, expressionist kind of door. No door at all. A silvered floor for some reason and a barrier so the actors could pretend to be in a steelworks. And how were the actors going to exit and enter? They were all going to be sitting on seats round the floor. I couldn't believe it. Keep the words, I thought. Just keep the fuckin' words.

Being involved in a bad theatrical experience is a bit like dropping acid. After an hour or two, you can't say, 'I think I'd rather do something else.' You're committed. It's like boxing. You can't say you'd really rather not fight the night. You've got to go down the line with it even though it's a horrible strain. Try sitting in this rehearsal room being a football manager who's not allowed to shout for ages, and ages. I felt like an arrogant asshole as far as Wee Ben was concerned. The play was full of people doing smack and rolling joints and Wee Ben had never taken drugs. He had a different view. Classic fuck-up coming up. Everybody wasn't doing the same play. I wished I was somewhere else. I got drunk one day and fell asleep on the benches at the back of the theatre. Snoring throughout.

It didn't stop them asking me a second time. I was cheap.

I was so cheap. If I hadn't been broke, I'd have told them to fuck off. I was broke because Radio Scotland didn't want to do *Bombed*, the one about blowing up Maggie Thatcher. So there was Wee Ben sitting in my kitchen. I couldn't keep the grin off my face. Wee Ben did not want to be sitting in my kitchen. Why was he sitting there? His boss had sent him. I don't know why. Maybe it was be rotten to Wee Ben time. He asked if I had any ideas. People who control what drama you see or hear do not ask you where you get your ideas from. They just want to know if you've got any. You're then supposed to make a pitch. If you look convincing during this part of the conversation, you might get them to give you some money eventually. It's how you look when you talk to them that's most important. They won't have a clue if your idea is any good or not. Even when they read the script they probably won't know. That's one of the reasons why so much new drama you see is complete shite. The people who get the jobs deciding what you can see or hear didn't get tested on scripts to see if they should get these jobs. How they look and sound to the people who are inter-viewing them is probably most important.

When Wee Ben asked if I'd any ideas, I told him I had a wonderful idea. In fact, I had a wonderful script. I knew it was a wonderful script. Even though when I tried to talk to anyone in Radio Scotland about it they all seemed to have gone on a hand-washing holiday to Australia. Wee Ben did a great job on it as well. Watching something you've written work well in front of an audience is about as good as it gets. But I suppose if you did it all the time it would begin to pall a little.

It didn't pall with Mora after the delirious first dog fuck.
She started coming back round to the flat then, supposedly
still for a shower. Except she'd come about lunchtime and
Jerry never got back till after five. We'd have a cup of
coffee. It became almost a ritual beginning. Then let the
screwing commence. She was wonderful, always in a good
mood during the breaks. She seemed to spend a lot of
time lolling on the couch with her legs open. This
intrigued me. I'd never been with anyone who never
seemed to close their legs. It drew attention to itself. It
drew you in. It transfixed. Sometimes it seemed to be the
only thing in the room. Sometimes it seemed to be
the only difference between us.

When I first moved into South Clerk Street, I'd just
started buying dirty books. I reckoned I didn't like dirty
books because I'd been brought up a Catholic. I imagined
I might be getting into dirty books as a liberating gesture,
but if you get into amphetamine sulphate you can wank
yourself to a frazzle over hours and hours and hours, and
maybe that's why I got into the dirty books. So it's 1976
and I'm opening this dirty book.

'Whit's that?' I said to this guy I knew.

'That's a cunt, Matt,' he said matter-of-factly.

'Since when have they had open cunts in dirty maga-
zines?' I asked, amazed that I could buy this off the top
shelf in the local newsagent.

Years before this I read a novel once that said they were
all the same, more or less. Completely retarded my sexual
development, that. Couldn't pull that one on many fifteen-
year-old schoolboys these days. Of course, they don't look

the same. Even the same one won't look the same if you stare at it long enough.

~~~~~~~~~~~~~~~~~~~~~~~~~

We still didn't talk much. We didn't listen to the radio. We didn't play the stereo. She sucked a lot. Every time it went down, she blew it back up again. We fucked a lot. We seemed to spend a lot of time in a very good mood. Whatever we said to each other usually lacked much significance. Then she said something very odd out of the blue.

'It's better to be a slave than a master,' she said.

'Whit?' Sometimes your eyes have to open wide.

'The slave does everything. The master just thinks he's in control. A master is nothing without a slave. A slave doesn't need a master. A master needs a slave.' It sounded like a manifesto.

'Where did ye read that?' I said.

'It might have been Hegel,' she said. She smiled. It was the only time she mentioned anything even mildly intellectual. She might have thought I was too stupid to understand. I didn't understand what she was on about with this master and slave stuff. We'd just been fucking all over various items of furniture and then it just popped out. Did it simply mean it's better to be a slave. Or did it mean I'd like to be a slave? Or did it mean I am a slave? It made me look at her a little differently.

I can only ever remember talking to her about orgasms. If you spent almost all your time with a person shagging and fucking and riding each other, it seemed to me a reasonable topic of conversation. She said it was like a warm glow. She made it sound like an advert for Ovaltine or Porridge Oats.

I read a book about it once. It was this dirty book by this dead liberated woman all about women wanking. They'd filled in a questionnaire to say how they'd been wanking, how they'd done it, how often, etc., so the author could produce some spurious statistics and pretend to be a social scientist. So many per cent wanked in the bath. Warm water, no clothes on, rubbing yourself all over, not much of a surprise there. So many per cent of the percentage who wanked in the bath used a faucet. A what? A faucet. I had to look up a dictionary to reassure myself. A faucet is a tap. A bath tap in this instance. How does one masturbate with a bath tap? How does one get up to it or down to it? I asked a friend of mine once and she didn't want to talk about it. If this book ever gets published, I'd like someone to write and tell me how it's done. The tap can't be on. The water would be too hot or too cold. But the book was American. Perhaps they have different plumbing arrangements in America. Perhaps they have taps like long nozzles which pop off the porcelain at the given moment and vibrate towards you sounding like a motor boat.

They had a film of a woman having an orgasm on the TV recently. They'd managed to get a miniature TV crew up her somehow. It came on when I was in the pub with some nephews. People were craning their necks. I didn't see it because a crowd formed in front of me and I was pretending to be too cool to stand up. But I knew it wasn't going to tell me anything anyway. If you can't experience it, you might be able to measure it. Blood, breath, nerve endings. You can measure someone having a ski jump, but that won't give you much insight into what it's like to be flying through the air, hundreds of feet up, without any wings to flap.

Just a slight difference in hormones and women might as well be Martians. When it comes to sex, I've probably got more in common with a chimpanzee than I have with a woman. If a male chimpanzee could speak, he'd probably say an orgasm was a bit like Ugh, Ugh, Whoosh! A female chimpanzee (don't tell me the poor things don't have orgasms!) would probably say it was a bit like an Ovaltine advert. Male chimpanzees have harems, of course. You get to have a harem because you can fight.

If you're a male chimpanzee, the bigger you are probably the better it is. This is the law of the jungle. Big monkeys biff wee monkeys. So I find myself in this boxing ring with this guy in Shotts and I must be giving away nearly two stone. I hadn't been sparring much and agreed to go and fight on the usual short notice. This is a list of excuses. I'd gone deaf in one ear as well. I still had both legs. Could have done with my ears getting syringed, though. You really don't need to have anything wrong with you before a fight. It preys on your mind. Even tiny little things. Like the possibility of getting whacked full on the earhole when it's blocked with wax. What would that be like? The horror of blood and wax running down your neck. And we're not talking about a little bit of wax here. There's yards of the stuff in there. It's not really wax either. Not like beeswax. More like shite. Blood and shite running down your neck and everyone fainting around you. Perforated eardrums. No swimming off the coral reefs for you, sonny boy.

I told myself I wouldn't have to listen for the bastard whoever he was. And there he was. Two-Ton Tony. It gets silly. You can't back up someone who's almost two stone heavier than you, not if you're a welterweight. Not by just shoving and leaning on them. When I blocked a punch I still got knocked back three feet. Not that I blocked many. Every now and again I'd see this huge arm begin to swing and in slow motion the gloved fist would loom larger, then Karump!

I moved away when I got hit. I knew what I was supposed to do. I'd had five fights by then. I was the fittest I ever was in a boxing ring. And I knew what I was supposed to do. I was very clear-headed except for four or five times in the first round when these huge slow blows whacked off the top off my head, or my forehead, or off my temple. I couldn't seem to stop him bouncing me all around the ring. Then the referee stopped it.

A drop of blood landed on my eyelash. The ref was looking at my eyebrow. I was delighted. I was going to get stopped with a cut eye. I'd never been stopped with a cut eye before. Something new every day.

'Ith it hut?' I said.

'Jist a graze. Box on,' he replied, stepping out the way so I could get a full view of Two-Ton Tony who was standing there beating his fists together, waiting.

I'd have been better just to keep out the bastard's road, but you've got to try and show willing somehow when all these people are screaming for the guy to knock you out. I tried something different. When he barged into me, I got my head down and slung in a right uppercut to the solar plexus. Nothing to drop a big boy like him. It held him up for a second or two maybe. I was getting battered and cuffed all around the head during this, by the way.

Boing! Boing! It was hard to keep your balance with all this weight banging into you. My feet weren't planted right. The second time was better. The third time he came in I caught him again. That was a good one. My feet were planted and I got there well before he did. Most of the crowd didn't know what that was like, but me and the big boy had an inkling. The crowd must have wondered why he was going back, but I knew he wanted a rest. Solar plexus punches, even if they're not hard enough to sink you, are fucking horrible. Ding ding. End of round one. I felt quite good going back to the corner. The guy was retreating at the end of the round. He looked a bit puffed. I didn't feel tired in the slightest. I think I felt like I'd escaped from a bear pit. Quite exhilarated somehow.

'How's the eye?' I said.

'Just grazed,' said the man.

I was so pleased to get back to my stool it was a real shame when the bell went again. But I knew something. I couldn't stop the guy hitting me. He was bludgeoning through my guard and biffing me all over the ring whether I had my hands up or not. But he was slow. He was just too big. I couldn't trade blows with this guy. Three thumping punches to the head at the start of round two. Fuck this! I dropped my guard. I decided to be Sugar Ray Leonard. I was going to confuse the lugubrious fucker. I could see his eyes flickering as he tried to work this one out. Moved to the left and caught him with a left jab coming up from the waist. Nice one. Not quite point of the chin. Didn't see it coming. Didn't seem to bother him, though. But he seemed to have stopped for a second or two. I don't think he knew where to look when my hands weren't sticking up in front of my face. Hit him again. Same punch. Moving to the left, then moving in. Left

again. I think I was getting quite excited. He hadn't hit
back.

The spontaneous action occurs from the clear mind. You
do the thing you're going to do without thinking about it
at all. You don't know you're going to do it. But you can
do it because you've practised it a thousand times on heavy
bags, and you've seen it on the TV, and you've done it in
your head. But if you've never done it to a real live person
before, and haven't even thought about doing it, nobody's
going to be as surprised as you are.

Left as I moved in. And right. Somebody threw it. It came
up from the waist and caught him square on the side of
the jaw. The shock went right up my arm. His head turned
to face leftwards. His body seemed to turn very slowly
after it and I was falling back towards the ropes when his
legs gave way and he crashed to his knees. The way
his body spun round was the strangest thing to see. I was
staring, amazed, in the neutral corner. The boy was on
his hands and knees. The ref was counting him out. Seven.
No, the bastard was trying to get up! I was thinking stay
down. Stay down. Stay fucking down! I'd knocked him
down and the bastard was getting up! I couldn't believe
it. Nine. And he's up. Beat the count. I knew he'd kill me
in the third if he managed to get over this. 'Box on,' says
the referee.

I knew I had to get him out of there. I swarmed all over

him. I hit him the full length of the ring. I had not the slightest morsel of pity for him in my entire body. He'd dished it out and now he was going to have to soak it up if I had anything to do with it. He came off the far rope and I closed on him again near the middle of the ring. Up close. Head down. A big red-vested torso. Left right, left right to the ribs. You could nearly feel it take the heart out of him. His arms came down as they do. Left right to the head. He staggered back. I caught up with him again. Left right to the head. It knocked him back on to the ropes again. His head kind of lolled back and the referee shouted, 'Stop!' The referee shouted stop. The head came forward. For the first, last and only time I hit someone with the right uppercut to the chin. Smacked him just right and sent his head back again. The referee was pulling me off.

I hadn't heard him shouting stop. He was shouting into my deaf ear. Even if I hadn't had a deaf ear, I probably wouldn't have heard him. I was in killing mode. I was moving with as much consciousness as a shark in a feeding frenzy. There was no pity. There was no empathy. I was treating him like a lump of meat.

That's what pornography's about, isn't it? Treating people like lumps of meat. Or looking at them as if they were lumps of meat. Somehow you look at them as if there wasn't a person there. You've taken the person away. You can look at them differently. If you tie their hands together, they really are in your power.

Somehow it's the best thing about fighting, when you
don't think and you don't care. When you move along on a
flow of concentration and spontaneous violence, a violence
which doesn't ask if this is right or wrong. And nobody
else watching will be asking these questions either.
Everyone who wasn't with the big boy loved it. It was a
good fight. A dwarf against an ogre. Everybody knows it's
better when the dwarf wins.

I wakened up that night about four in the morning. I
always did that after fights, no matter what had happened.
I always wakened up with a sore head. I assumed this was
brain damage. I had no problem with that. I assumed
hangovers were brain damage as well. The reason why
your head is sore inside is obviously because it's been
damaged. But that night was unusual. The sorest thing
about me was my right forearm. The whole bone. I could
feel it. I couldn't have thrown a harder punch. If the boy
had been the same weight as me there was no way he
would have beaten the count. I didn't like that. What's it
like when you don't even hear the count? When you're
lying there and your leg's twitching and they're waving
smelling salts under your nose? You could become just
another regrettable incident.

After she said the stuff about the master and slave, I
phoned her up one morning. I'd been up all night,
speeding. I'd been thinking about fucking and riding and

shagging and tying people up for hours. I wanted to try it. I wanted to realise the fantasy.

'If ye come round today, Ah'm goiny, uh, blindfold ye an' tie ye up,' I said. I was staring out the window of the phone box with big, saucer eyes. I didn't feel as if it was me standing there. The voice on the other end of the phone seemed a hundred million miles away.

'What?' she was giggling.

'Ah've been thinkin' about it all night,' I said in an oddly choked voice. I swallowed hard. 'Uh, maybe you'd better not come.'

'Why not?'

'Ah'm goiny, uh, tie ye up,' I said.

'Tie me up then,' she said.

chapter eight

There can't be more than a couple of chapters of this
book left. What will I do after that? I'll have to go through
it again and make corrections, of course, but I'm not going
to bother re-writing it, and re-writing it, and re-writing
it like I usually do. But this book's been really quick. I
started it in August and I'm only half-way through January
now. I could be finished in a month, just after my forty-
fourth birthday. The last time I wrote a novel from
scratch, it took me two and half years. It was all about
this little Middle Eastern kingdom getting attacked by this
big Middle Eastern kingdom. Of course, the Middle East
wasn't mentioned in the novel. That did not stop Saddam
Hussein starting the Gulf War right after I'd worked out
the plotline. Actually, it was an archetypal hero myth epic,
a sand and sandals saga with geopolitical and religious
overtones. No wonder nobody wanted to publish it.

The first thing I'll do after I've finished this is give it to
the Lonesome Cowboy, Bill Campbell. He and Peter
McKenzie own Mainstream Publishing. I'd give it to
Peter, but he said the sand and sandals epic didn't have
enough adjectives in it. I'll phone up Lonesome Cowboy
Bill and tell him I've written this book about fighting and
fucking, a cross between Charles Bukowski, Henry Miller,
Jeannette Winterson and Kurt Vonnegut. That'll throw

him. He won't have heard of at least two of those people.
I can say what I like about him. He won't have read it
this far. They won't publish this, but that's probably just
as well. I wouldn't want my mother to read it. I wouldn't
like the kids in the school where I work to read it either.
I've never written a dirty book in the first person, or any
other kind of dirty book for that matter. I've spent a long
time trying to write really good paragraphs. Here's one.

'A rich man's whim, a converted paddle-steamer known
as the *Christopher*, rounded the headland and, adjusting its
course, slid through the still waters and began to approach
the quayside. At the end of a short voyage which seemed,
like others before it, lacking in purpose, it travelled
without cargo or hope of profit. Ever since Angus had
stopped the money going into the railroad, manoeuvres
were made without meaning on journeys between civilis-
ation and nothing very much at all.'

I re-wrote that at least thirteen times. Was dying to re-
write it. Too many commas. It's from a novel about a guy
who goes into a cave for six years, does his yoga and
meditation, floats spontaneously, i.e., up into the air
and round about, and tries to become president of the
United States around the year 2000. Once you removed
the prose you had a radio play. It got a great review
in the *Scotsman*. 'Dramatic coup', 'Witty and intelligent',
etc. Never worked for the radio again. When it was
getting made in London, I had this meeting with a guy
from Fontana. He'd bought the paperback rights to a
novel I got published.

He didn't want the book about the boy floating about. That did not matter. He'd just published the other one and told me that what I needed to do was produce one like that every eighteen months. When I'd had four of them published, I might start making some money. I asked if he wanted books the same as the one he'd just published. Not exactly the same. But kind of the same, quite like it, anyway. One every eighteen months so the booksellers didn't forget your name. If I'd been writing full-time, I could have knocked off a book sort of the same as the one I got published in six months. No bother. Two-thirds of my time I could have spent doing what I liked. I had to tell him I was sorry, of course. Terribly sorry. I was looking after my baby daughter at the time and I could only find two hours a day to write in. If I started writing a book sort of the same as the one I got published, I reckon I could have finished it in three years. Maybe four. I suppose it took me thirteen years to get to that lunch. Thank God I didn't have to pay for it.

I wrote the book I got published when I was still living with Jerry. When I finished writing the book about the steelworks, Poisonous and the Assistant Head told me it was crap and that I should try to write a sci-fi, something with a plot in it anyway. So I worked out my first plotline and fantasised about having a paperback book on the racks at Waverley Station.

I had a great routine when I was re-writing that novel. I

used to come home from my work and run four miles. Then I'd have something to eat and write for two hours or so. Around nine o'clock, I'd stagger stoned out of the tiny kitchen where I worked, and watch the TV. I worked about four hours every Saturday and Sunday. I had school holidays then. I used to watch the sun shining down outside the kitchen window. When the holidays were over and I went back to work, at first I didn't believe I could keep up a routine like that. Completely straight, it would have been impossible.

Four years later the book was still crap. Lonesome Cowboy Bill asked me if I'd anything else on the go. I told him I was doing a radio play based on the book he'd rejected seven or eight years earlier. He asked to read it again. He said he was going to publish it. 'You can't publish that,' I think I said. 'I'll have to re-write it.' 'You've got three weeks,' he said.

I had a great routine when I was re-writing that novel. It was during the Easter holidays. I used to get up in time for 'The World at One'. I'd work after that through till twelve o'clock at night, stopping only to stick food into my face. Then I'd start drinking bottles of Guinness around midnight. When I was too drunk to operate my typewriter any more, I went to bed. Then I got up in time for 'The World at One'. I put the novel through the typewriter, took the swearing out of the dialogue, and purpled up the prose here and there in about ten days. They needed it in three weeks because of some Scottish Arts Council committee meeting. I thought I'd have time to re-write it properly when the Scottish Arts Council told them to fuck off, but the next thing I saw was the final proofs.

Those boys didn't keep in the business of publishing in Scotland throughout the black night of the fascist regime by being assholes and throwing their money around. I don't think Peter cares how many adjectives you use. The name of the game is to make money. As Andy Warhol said, somebody's got to bring home the bacon. You can't go around publishing people just because you're related to them unless you're rich already and don't mind losing some money.

If you want to get books published, you've got to make yourself worth exploiting. I used to think about this when I was pushing the babe around in the buggy. I'd take the kid up to the dole office and then push her down Princes Street and into Waverley Station. There I'd see the paperback and I'd pull out some copies and cover up the front of other books with them. That always put me in a good mood, even though nobody was daft enough to buy my book anyway. But you've got to be ruthless. It's a dog-eat-dog world out there.

At least I had a book published. Radio Scotland were going to give me four grand, I was sure, for the play about the boy floating about. I was finding out how to screw a writer's bursary out of the Scottish Arts Council. I was going to give up work and write full-time for a whole year. And I could live well for a whole year. I'd have time to write a couple of books and live the life of Riley before I had to think about money at all. I was going to be as happy as a pig in shit. What a routine I was going to have! Running and shadow boxing, writing at leisure and getting stoned out of my tree every night. But my girlfriend did not seem keen on me giving up my secure but meagrely paid pseudo-professional little post. When I asked her why, she told me she was pregnant. That's how I became a housewife instead of a famous writer of books which were sort of kind of the same, but not quite.

I should have been ruthless. I should have said, pregnant? Oh, really? I'll have to move out. Won't be able to work if you've got a baby crying all over the place. Besides, I'll have to spend some time in Birmingham. I've been asked to help write 'The Archers', you know.

People think I'm having them on when I tell them that. But it's true. I was asked if I wanted to help write 'The Archers'. I want it on my tombstone. Dum de dum de dum de dum, dum de dum de di dee. I could have been a contender, Charlie. But what did I get? A one-way ticket to Palukaville. Or, in my case, the Broxburn Rangers Supporters Club.

When Wee Benny told me he was going to take me to fight at the Broxburn Rangers Supporters Club, I told him that might not be such a good idea. I knew what

Rangers supporters were like. Rangers supporters were Orange bastards. I knew what Orange bastards were like because when I was about seven I discovered what Orange Walks are. Orange Walks are when some white trash, the proverbial proto-fascist scum, the dregs, triumphantly tell people they don't even know how much they hate them. And I was a Rangers supporter as well. When I was seven Rangers won everything, just like they do today. I could name the team even now. Because supporting winners made sense to me even then, I was a Rangers supporter till I was told I couldn't be a Rangers supporter because all the other supporters were Orange bastards who hated me. Even though they didn't even know me. And I was only seven years old at the time.

When I told Wee Benny I was brought up a Catholic, he said not to worry about that. He was brought up a Catholic as well. Billy the Trainer was brought up a Catholic, although he was called Billy. Danny the Flyweight wasn't called Daniel O'Connell, but it was close. I checked it out. Only one of the fighters with us was brought up a Prod and he was a Hearts supporter.

Everyone should visit the Broxburn Rangers Supporters Club at least once in their life. Everything was red, white and blue. The wallpaper was red, white and blue. Even the table tops were red, white and blue. The place was full of men with greasy black hair and long sideburns. You could tell them a mile away, either Orange bastards or Elvis impersonators. And, of course, they were all very nice. That was stunning. They were just like me. I kept wanting to say, 'I'm a Celtic supporter, by the way.' Faith of our fathers and all that. But it's better sometimes to keep your trap shut. It was like being with a bunch of old Germans. Everything will be fine as long as you don't mention the war.

It wasn't at the Broxburn Rangers Supporters Club that I had my last fight. It was just down the road from where I'm sitting just now. At Tiffany's, once the dance hall where I went with Mora, now a hole in the ground. I didn't want to fight. It was about six months after the fight I had in Shotts and I didn't want to fight. I wanted to go watch the fights and get drunk with my pals. Maybe there was a gap in the bill. I don't know. Maybe Wee Benny wanted to get me back into fighting regularly. Who knows? I was told I'd get £10 for expenses and that would pay my half of the rent for a fortnight.

Ten pounds for half a flat for a fortnight was cheap even then. The woman who owned the flat was the best land-lady in the world. The rent would have just about covered the mortgage if she'd still being paying one. She was not exploiting us much. All landlords, even those who just own one flat, don't have to be bastards. It's just that most of them are.

I was fighting a dwarf. I'd been to the Lake District on holiday just before the fight, drinking and smoking fags, eating like a pig. I was fat. The boy I was fighting didn't look too slim either, but he must have been at least half a stone lighter than me. Before going into the ring, I wasn't particularly nervous. I just didn't want to be there. I thought, why am I here? I'm twenty-nine years of age. I don't need this shit. I felt pretty scunnered beforehand, and the first round didn't help. All I had to do was stand there in the middle of the ring and wait for the wee boy to walk on to straight lefts. I was too out of shape to think about chasing him. It was enough just to stand there. I wasn't properly engaged. I didn't like the way his head kept jerking back. I had a really solid straight left by then. When the bell went for the end of the first, the straight lefts I'd landed on the boy were probably bothering me more than him. Billy the Trainer told me to chin him. Left then right uppercut. He said, chin him and get him out of there.

I went out and danced around the boy. I moved back. I made him miss. I didn't look at my corner. I let him come at me, then moved away. I wasn't fit enough to do that for two minutes. When I stopped, we scuffled. I was tired. I got hit too much. We probably halved the round. The people in my corner were not pleased with me after the second round. They knew I was blowing it. It wasn't to teach me this that they showed up at training three times a week. The third round and I'm just dying for it to come to an end. There is nothing as horrible as fighting when you're not fit for it. When the pall of cigarette smoke starts three inches above your head and your lungs are burning sore and you just want out of this rather off-colour, tawdry little scene. I knew it hadn't long to go. I was lasting out, losing the round, but I'd won the first by a mile. Bang! I'm dumped on my arse. Left hook. We were in close and I never even seen it. A flash knockdown. Didn't hurt me, just pissed me off. I got up and the ref counted to eight. Box on. The bell went immediately. Unanimous decision to the dwarf in the blue corner. But you've got to be ruthless. A boxing ring is the last place to start taking pity on someone, because the last thing they're going to do is take pity on you. I shook the boy's hand and told him it was a good decision. I knew I was never going to step into a boxing ring again.

I'd had it all. Eight fights. Won five, lost three. Apart from the last dwarf, the other two were southpaws. Never did beat a southpaw. But I got it all. Knocked down some guys. Some guys knocked me down. I got stopped in the first round. I stopped some other guy in the first round. I took a standing count. I gave some guy a standing count. I'd been good and I'd stunk the place out. I'd had two black eyes. One of my thumbs regularly ballooned up after every other fight. Once, I couldn't hit a bag with my left for over a year because of a sore shoulder. A damaged knee ligament kept me off the roads for something like eighteen months. After every fight I had a headache. After the last fight I was standing in the bogs at Tiffany's trying to snort up some coke through nostrils that were clogged with blood. Going into the boxing club at Meadowbank Stadium was certainly the best thing I ever did in my life, but it gets to be like sex when you stand back and think, what else can I have when I've had everything I'm going to get?

There was just going to be more of the same. Maybe with

me and Mora it had come to the stage it was bound to come to after a couple of months of the feelie-gropey stuff. Nobody lives in the white heat of passion for ever. After a couple of months, it'll get as boring as everything else. Maybe long ago your caveman captured somebody and banged her for three months and then let her go. By then the somebody would be pregnant, of course. I don't suppose cavemen talked about much, either. But it's a natural span, this two or three months. After that maybe even a caveman would want to come up for some air.

And I thought it had got her over the crazy stuff. She didn't talk about killing Doreen any more. She hadn't mentioned Doreen for weeks, although I knew she'd passed her driving test. Jerry was still being offhand in a nice kind of way and she still smiled and smiled and smiled in a way that was weird to me. But she didn't weep. That was the main thing. She hadn't wept for ages and ages. Having sex with her was much, much better than having to put up with that for hours at a stretch. Anything was better than that. Maybe she didn't cry any more because she was getting her revenge by sleeping with me. It gave me a strange feeling when I realised she'd let me do anything I wanted to do. That's not how you have relationships with people, even cavemen. You've got to leave some room for negotiation. Some give and take. Maybe keep something back for special occasions. But just when you think the life's just about to go out of something, what comes along but a bit of a stimulant.

There's nothing like taking amphetamine sulphate to set

you up for some satiation, followed of course by the *grand ennui*. I found out all about amphetamine sulphate from the Forth Valley Health Board. They produced a set of slides to teach schoolchildren about speed. Bound to be out of date now, but it said there were three main kinds of amphetamines. Starting from the best down, there was methedrine, dexedrine and amphetamine sulphate, otherwise known as benzedrine. Amphetamine sulphate is Jack Kerouac country. Hitler was into methedrine. That's why he declared war on the United States when he'd no reason to. We used to take dexedrine at university. There was a picture of a student on the slides. This student was obviously still a committed member of various trainspotting associations, but he took speed to help him study. But afterwards, as the next slide showed, he looked pretty fed up, depressed and completely knackered. That was just like us boys when we were students. It was only when the government stopped making dexedrine that amphetamine sulphate appeared. They stopped making dexedrine partly because housewives were discovered hanging out of buildings vigorously cleaning their windows at four o'clock in the morning. They should have left well alone. Though not necessarily always, amphetamine sulphate is usually a bit of a rabid dog.

But I suppose it depends if your mind turns that way. I thought we'd reached a kind of limit, Mora and I, until Poisonous hustled some speed to me. I answered the door dressed in my lab coat. I wasn't wearing anything else. I pulled her inside. She was giggling.

chapter nine

I can't be bothered doing that dirty bit tonight. I keep wondering what I'll do when I finish writing this. Hope springs eternal. Last year I had my four novels rejected by every publisher in Britain. Every publisher in Britain. When I finish this maybe I should write to every agent in Britain. I could get rejected by every agent and every publisher in Britain. Then I could go global. Get rejected by every publisher in Hong Kong, even the ones who only publish menus.

One of these days by a great cosmic accident I will be standing at last on the high ground looking down on these bastards. I'll be selling as many books as Jeffrey Archer. I'll write to publishers and ask if I can join their lists. I can see all the salivating dyslexic bastards now. Then I'll reject them. Dear Crap Books Ltd., I do not wish to be associated with your business since your grovelling letter did not have enough adjectives in it.

What would be really great would be to have a book

accepted and then decide not to have it published. Nobody does that. Everyone wants to become something. I'm too old now to become something. I'd just like the bastards to give me some money for enjoying myself at that time of night when there's nothing else to do. The only good reason for getting something published is to make money. If I get this book published, I might get a grand. If I only had a grand, I could be a millionaire! I know a guy who's had four books published and he hasn't got two pennies to rub together. But hope springs eternal. If I make some money out of this book, I've promised to go along the road through the Nullarbor Plain.

The Nullarbor Plain is really a big desert. It sort of joins east and west Australia. Driving across it takes days. Only roadhouses dot the highway. I've promised myself I'll go into the desert near one of the roadhouses towards the middle. I want to camp out on my own and examine the contents of my mind. I asked my daughter if she'd come and visit me and she said, 'Why would I want to visit you?' The only way I'm going to get under that beautiful big blue Australian sky is if people like reading dirty books. Maybe you need the contents of your mind examined if you can write dirty books like this.

Mora giggled as I pulled her through the door of the flat. I was wearing my lab coat. Nothing else. I spun her round and blindfolded her with a black scarf. Then I led her along the hall and into the living room. She was still giggling. 'Let me introduce Brutus, the German shepherd dog,' I shouted. I tied her hands behind her back, using bandages from the boxing. Then I pushed her back on to the couch and pulled off her tights and knickers. I hauled her back on to her feet and introduced several other men who weren't there, and she was still giggling. It sounded very carefree and trusting. You could tell she wasn't expecting anything bad to happen to her. I led her into the kitchen and got her to bend over to snort up the last of the speed. I lifted her skirt and had two fingers up her before she pulled her head away from the mirror. It was ten o'clock in the morning. We had all day.

Amphetamine sulphate will make you impotent. Your willie will shrivel up and your goolies will try to climb back into your body. Amphetamine sulphate will make you impotent, but amphetamine sulphate mixed with glucose and baby milk and horse laxatives will not make you all that impotent. Even if you manage to snort up enough to make your willie shrivel up, it won't shrivel up for ever, or even for very long. And when it goes erect, it will stay erect for ages and ages. Premature ejaculation on amphetamine sulphate is about three hours later. This gives you plenty of time to get round to the things you might not normally have time to get round to.

But you must never get frustrated. You must never lose yourself in a frenzy of wanting to come, because the other person will probably get sore and you might not be able to come anyway. You must feel as if above it. Though your eyes may be popping and the sweat lashes off you, you've still got to try and relax. Otherwise the whole thing might get a little bit fraught. I was banging her backwards as she bent over the table and I told myself I'd better cool it. I took her into the living room. I was gasping and sweat was dripping on to the carpet already. We tried to figure out how to get her smock off with her hands behind her back. She giggled again. I undid the bandages and tied her hands at the front. I didn't want to take off the blindfold.

It's odd when you put a blindfold on someone. You kind of lose them. A huge part of them kind of disappears. You can look at them differently. It's like being intimate with someone who isn't all there somehow. You can look at them as if they're an object. They're partly dehumanised. That must be why they blindfold people before they shoot them. They're in your power. It's a power trip. Not always necessarily a prelude to something sado-masochistic. Definitely somewhere on the submission/domination graph, though. But what are you supposed to do with someone when they're tied up and blindfolded and ready for some bondagey sex games? The first thing you're supposed to do is make sure they have lots of orgasms. It's up to them. You'll do anything. But if they won't tell you what to do, you might as well do what you want. I lifted her arms up in the air and pulled the smock up to her chin, but not over her head. I'd lost her head. Then I laid her down on the couch and screwed her for at least an hour. It was hard to say. I was very focused, as one would be on amphetamine sulphate, but not on the time. I tried to match the screwing to the breathing I heard coming through the smock. I stared and stared at her body and mine. But I didn't come. I didn't want to come.

The last thing you really want to do is come. All the riding and fucking and shagging, and even making love, is bound to come to a stop when you come. Coming is a bit of a no-no, though you're eventually going to want to come sometime. That's probably because you've been told that coming's the whole point of the business. You're conditioned into thinking that you should come, but after you come you're not going to be having as good a time as you were just previously. *Post coitum omnia animalia tristia sunt.* That's the only Latin I know apart from *festina lente*. I'll be ramming in the only verse of poetry I know soon. The Latin means that after you hanky panky you're going to be pissed off. I think some people have had a go at addressing this problem.

If you're a Taoist, to be really healthy what you need is about ten young women between the ages of fourteen and nineteen. Just imagine you managed to find ten cooperative young women who looked a bit like a seventeen-year-old Brigitte Bardot. What you're supposed to do is go to bed with these people one after the other, engage in penetrative sex and not come. When you're about to come, you're supposed to withdraw and grab the part between your goolies and your asshole, called your perineum, thus preventing ejaculation. No mention was made in the book where I read this about whacking your erection with the heel of your shoe, but this might help. Could be a Friday night spectacular on satellite TV. Miniature TV crews up everyone to check for cheating and let's see who's the Taoist bonking champion for this week.

It doesn't say what you get out of this stuff if you're a lady Taoist. I guess you're just supposed to open your legs and stare at the wall. No change there. But the phallocentric psychoanalyist who reckoned coitus interruptus is bad for you should have worked something out with these Taoist people. A middle way, maybe. Like leave out the shoe.

Then there was this shaman boy in the *Scotsman* the other week. He says he doesn't come. He says he directs his sperm up his spine and has an internal orgasm, like a woman, he says. This is the boy for me. I even think I've got an idea of what he might be talking about, although he should definitely cut the sperm talk out of his remarks to the press. Maybe something white, a bit like you'd imagine something like sperm, may be going up what you might imagine to be your spine. Maybe you can even imagine the warm, glowing mug of Ovaltine while you're about it.

I don't know where this shaman boy learnt his stuff, but I read once that the shaman of the Innuit could go to the moon to pick up babies for lady Innuit with fertility problems. The woman with the fertility problems had to sleep with the shaman, of course. That was the deal. She sleeps with the shaman and he goes to the moon. The Innuit apparently did not believe you could get pregnant by sleeping with someone just once. This is a wonderfully liberating thing to believe in. I think everyone should believe in that, even though it's not true. Probably nothing people believe in is true anyway, so the Innuit at least picked on something that gives everyone a break. Maybe they thought it took months to get the belly pumped up.

~~~~~~~~~~

You wouldn't put a bicycle pump up someone and blow air into them, would you? Not even if you'd hours of sex on your hands and had never done that before. No, you wouldn't do that. Not even if you were out of your head on amphetamine sulphate. I'll leave it out, anyway. As well as the stuff about the ice cubes.

~~~~~~~~~~

I kind of came to myself and stopped for a moment. My eyes flicked around. I listened intently. She was still gasping. The tap was dripping in the kitchen. There didn't seem to be another sound. Then I came out of her. I sat back on the edge of the couch and looked at her headless body. I spread her legs out a bit wider and then pushed her thighs apart as wide as I could get them. I stared at her cunt and stroked my palm slowly down it. She was all cunt. It seemed a huge part of her. I pulled the smock down a bit so that her head appeared again. Her face glistened with sweat and her hair was damp around the temples and wet at the nape of her neck. Her face seemed quite pale. We were talking. I wished I'd gotten the smock off earlier since it was going to get damp one way or another. I pulled it up her arms and it was held only by the bandages tying her hands. I left her there with the smock and stuff stretching over and on to the floor, her arms above her head, which was resting on the arm of the couch. I went for a towel to dry her off. Then I shut the curtains and put on the light. Then I put on the gas fire. I wanted it to be hot, sweaty and humid. Like the jungle.

....

When you take away the ejaculations flying all over the place, it's like sport. Maybe a cross between taking vigorous exercise and getting a blowjob. Cycles of bonking and dalliance. But it's the bit before you come that feels really nice. The writhing about in ecstasy, shoe in one hand and perineum clasped firmly in the other. Trying to reproduce that feeling time after time. But what feeling are we talking about here? Does it feel like a Porridge Oats advert or not? Not really. Hard to put it into words, though. Maybe it feels like what it feels like. Maybe I could sling in a few adjectives here to absolutely no avail.

....

I was staring at something I didn't understand. It was some time later. I was going to shave it. Don't try this at home, kids. If you've been doing the disco biscuits and you think you'd fancy a go at this, check carefully to see if your hands are shaking. You don't want to be shaking, or lose attention, or sneeze, or even breathe too much when the razor reaches towards the vertical. She asked me what I was doing when I started to soap her. I said I was going to shave her. She said 'Oh' in a soft voice. I was watching her hole. It tightened and slackened with the 'Oh'. I looked up at her face. The bottom jaw was kind of hanging. I was tempted to put my cock in her mouth, but tried to concentrate on the task at hand.

....

Not a nick. She said she wanted to look at it, but I wouldn't let her. I wanted to look at it myself. I wrote my name on it in Biro, with a rude message down either side. Then I got some vaseline and smeared it all over between her thighs and on to her lower belly. I put some on her asshole and a finger-length in. I'd bought the vaseline and some vegetables on the way back from the telephone kiosk. I tried her on a courgette. No, she did not recognise a courgette. Or a carrot. Or the start of a cucumber. I was licking her and fucking her with a candle, at the same time wishing I'd gone easier with the vaseline. But I thought she'd complain about becoming sore soon and I wanted it to last. I went for some cooking oil and poured some up her. I couldn't resist fucking her as hard as I could for a few minutes then. But I was going to come and had to stop again. I knelt her in front of the couch and sat on the towel she'd been sitting on. I pulled her head down on to my cock and stared at the wall for a while.

It was some time later. She was bent over this kind of footstool. The smock was on the carpet some way away and her hands were tied behind her back again. I was staring at her asshole. Was this going to be an abomination? Lord Byron's in-laws wouldn't let their daughter go back to him when she told them about all the buggering that was going on. Someone told me a wee while ago that it is against the law to bugger your wife. The amount of research I do. Once I read in the newspaper that forty-five per cent of Greek men bugger their wives as a form of contraception. Who makes up these statistics? So I was staring bug-eyed down at this asshole. That wasn't all I was doing. I was well into the rabid dog. I was kind of half wanking and half banging her. When I pulled it out to wank it harder, I'd push in the courgette and jiggle it around a little bit. I really liked the shape of that courgette. It was the most evocative vegetable I'd ever seen. But I was staring at her asshole and wondering if this might be pushing her a step too far.

I was speaking to a friend of mine about faggots recently. We were asking why anyone would dislike gay men. You might not be too sure what they're thinking sometimes when they're talking to you, but women have had to put up with that for ever. He said it was shite. He said people don't like the idea of buggery because of the shite. People think it's dirty, he said. Shite is dirty. People try their best to keep away from shite normally. I know what they feel like. Even a couple of years of changing nappies did not make me shite-friendly. I put up with the shite. I did not wash my hands in it or wipe it on my face. Apart from carrying horrible diseases, shite is probably okay. No, it's not. Shite's shite. I think gay men owe it to us straight people to do a publicity job on shite. A make-over. Banners reading SHITE IS NOT ALWAYS NECESSARILY INVOLVED or SHITE'S COOL.

So how far up does the shite start? Are we talking further than six inches here? How much shite is in there anyway? What is a colon? Just when I thought I'd given up using them, somebody says they're forty feet long and full of shite. Just that a bit drops off every now and again. This is all nonsense, of course, but how are we to know if no one tells us? Well, you can always try it out and see, I suppose.

It was nearly four o'clock in the afternoon. She was draped over the footstool, belly up. Sweat was running off the bottom of my chin and landing near her navel. There were bits of hair, fluff, dirt, grease, oil and vaseline sticking to us. The light seemed pinky yellow. A rivulet of sweat started just below her ribs and ran down to her neck. I could see only underneath her chin and not her face. I was going to come. I hadn't come for nearly three days. That was a long, long time then. I pulled it out of her and hauled her into a sitting position. I was hoping to stop the ejaculation, bending it a bit, gritting my teeth, but nothing was going to stop it this time. Whoosh! I was all over her face and neck. It didn't come in a spurt or a stream. It sprayed out. I'd never seen anything like it. It was almost clear, almost all semen. She said 'Ah' before her mouth squeezed round it and there was far too much of it again. She gagged and coughed and I pulled it clear again. It was still as hard as it ever was. I was panting and staring and shaking it again. There was more to come. Could hardly believe it. I pulled her half to her feet and turned her, pushed her down to her knees again, jammed it into her. And I was almost coming again when I pulled it out and slid it up her asshole.

I was asking someone about buggery a couple of weeks ago. I was asking them about the shite factor. They did not know where the shite started either, but they said gay men only put it in just past the knob. I couldn't believe that, especially if you were buggering someone wearing a condom as one is supposed to.

I slid it all the way in. I slid it in as far as it would go.
Couldn't think of any reason why not. Couldn't think at
all at the time. Had completely lost it. In the grip of a
wild thrusting passion. Then I shot what I thought was
the last of the spunk into her and took it out. I couldn't
believe it. It was still not finished. She was starting to
slide off the footstool on to the floor when I took her
again. Didn't feel guilty about ramming her arse as hard
as I could. It was her cunt that was sore. Then I was
sitting on the floor and kind of staring about in an awed
state of hyperventilation. She was lying flat out on the
carpet. Then she started getting up quite quickly. I was
so fucked I couldn't believe how quickly she was getting
up.

'Untie me! Untie me!' she said in an insistent yet
curious kind of way. She wasn't demanding. She wasn't
angry. I was suddenly scared she'd be furious, but she
wasn't. 'Come on, hurry up!' I pulled the bandages off her
wrists and she immediately pulled the scarf from her eyes.
I hadn't seen her eyes for hours and hours. They were
really shiny. It was as if another person had suddenly
jumped into Mora's skin. 'I want to see! I want to see!'
she said. There was a wall mirror just behind the footstool
and she turned and stepped in front of it.

'For fuck sake!' she said, totally uncharacteristically. 'I'm
covered in it! Covered in it! What a mess!' She was half-
way giggling and laughing, and half-way hysterical and
embarrassed. Some very rude remarks were written on
her belly and buttocks. She had no pubic hair left. 'Wha!
Wha!' she said as her eyes took in her reflection. Then
she skipped away towards the shower. 'My bum's sore!' she
said. she was leaning towards me and half bent over. She

seemed to be very amused by something. 'You perverted bastard! I'm going to write to your mother about this!'

I stared at her with my mouth hanging open. I thought she'd be furious. I thought she'd never speak to me again. I looked down at my cock and was just relieved that it wasn't covered in shite.

We were sitting in the wee kitchen a little later. We were showered, dressed and quite presentable. We were kind of nervous with each other. Or I was. We were kind of laughing in a half-embarrassed way. Or I was. Then I felt completely brain-dead. I'd been having a hard couple of days of it and really needed my bed. She said she still felt a bit speedy though she shouldn't have. She looked kind of up to me. Anybody would have. She said she was going home. I didn't mention her not waiting for Jerry. I thought Mora was a bit unsure about seeing him after she'd been taking drugs. She was weird that way. She looked straight enough to me. Anybody would have. But she'd never not waited to see Jerry before. I couldn't handle her without the blindfold. I wanted to blindfold her again. I was pleased to be rid of her when she said she was going for the bus.

I took her out to wait for the bus, then I went for a walk. I never went for walks. Walking's too slow. Everything takes too long. Walking's for moody bastards. I walked all the way round Arthur's Seat. I knew I was going to have to cool it with Mora. In some ways I wanted to cool it with Mora and in some ways I didn't. But it didn't look as if I'd much choice. The girlfriend was coming home from Australia. She loomed on the horizon like a black cloud. The thing with Mora would have to stop. I couldn't go on. After an afternoon like that, there wasn't much else I wanted to do with her anyway. I'd just find a reason not to phone her up. I walked round Arthur's Seat and I saw some ducks and that. I couldn't think of a reason not to phone her up. She was one of the wonderful people, after all.

Then I was getting shook awake. I'd been lying on the couch. It was one of those black pit sleeps. You close your eyes and the black pit envelops you. I must have dozed off on the couch. Jerry was offering me a bit of toast and a cup of coffee. I was still woozy when he started going on about Tracy. Tracy was coming round and I was supposed to screw her. I was moaning and groaning and holding my head as I walked around the room saying, 'No, oh no, oh no.' I was having a chat to Doreen just before the speed arrived to take lumps out of everything. She said Tracy wanted to screw somebody other than her boyfriend. Why? Just because. I said I'd screw her. This was a stupid thing to say. I didn't really want to screw her. But I said I would. I said I hadn't screwed her properly that first time and I'd like another shot at it. Even if I'd have wanted another shot some time later, I did not want one then. Not that night. Not after that day. I just went round the room saying, 'Oh no, oh no, oh no.' Jerry found all this very droll. He got me a coffee jar filled with home brew and started to roll a stick. He was smiling his big smile. It was okay for him.

We met them in the pub at the bottom of the road. Tracy seemed to be dressed up like Bud Flanagan. She was wrapped up in an old fur coat and had on a silly hat. I did not know what Doreen had said to her. I was hoping to sit there and have a couple of pints and keep a low profile. No chance. Doreen broached the subject right away. Tracy had told her boyfriend she was off to visit her sister who stayed out of town. Tracy was smiling at me with shiny eyes. Maybe they'd had a few drinks before they got there. She asked how my boxing was getting on. I'd forgotten all about it. She said that's why she wanted to get screwed by me. 'What?' I said. Because her boyfriend wasn't very aggressive. 'What do you mean?' She said she expected me to be a lot more aggressive than he was since I was a boxer. I was not a boxer, I told her. I sometimes went to boxing training. Boxers fought other boxers. I hadn't ever fought anyone at that point. 'But you know what I mean, don't you?' she said. I looked at her. She'd been to bed with me before. What was she talking about? Doreen and Jerry had started to talk among themselves. I was left staring at Tracy's face. I had no idea what she meant. 'What do you mean?' I said. 'Do you want me to be aggressive?' 'Yes,' she said. 'Kind of aggressive but not too rough, sort of.' Doreen rapped her on the elbow then to ask her something. I rolled my eyes at Jerry. Jerry smirked.

Back at the flat I plied everyone with home brew. Tracy and I didn't sit together or talk much. That was the usual. That was fine by me. I plied everyone with rotgut home brew. I was definitely getting drunk, even if no one else was. Then there were the sticks. We smoked a few of them. Tracy said she felt sick and staggered off out of the room. What a break! She'd got drunk and would now go and vomit, then crash out in the bedroom. That was fine. After another coffee jar of beer, I decided to follow her.

~~~~~~~~~~~~

She was totally awake, sitting up in bed, the sheet pulled up to her waist. The tits were out. It was showtime. I sat down on the edge of the bed and started to take my clothes off. My whole body was sighing. 'I don't know if I can handle this,' I think I said. 'How are you feeling?' She told me she'd thrown up, but she was fine now. What she really said was 'Ah vomited a while ago, but Ah'm ready fur it noo!' With that she spread her legs as she threw off the sheet. Such a display of *joie de vivre* I found difficult to comprehend. 'I don't know if I can handle this,' I muttered to myself. I pulled off my jeans and started to climb on to the bed. What can you say? Ah'm ready fur it noo! Where do they come from? But in that kind of light, with that kind of enthusiam, she did not look unattractive. A corpse might have got a hard-on climbing towards her like that. 'Your tits are brilliant. You're wet,' I think I said. 'Let's see if Ah can get it up ye.'

~~~~~~~~~~~~

She wasn't the kind of person who was going to move around a lot. She was going to lie there. Her hips seemed odd. It was as if she'd lie there, relax her hipbones and the joint kind of split, the pelvis or something. Pneumatic she wasn't. I lay on top of her and amused myself for as long as I could. There was no way I was going to come. I was three-quarters hard and that was as hard as it was going to get. After some time, I thought I'd hang her over the side of the bed and play with her tits. They were her best feature, after all. I started to haul her round. This woman was not a lightweight. I started to haul her round. 'Have you not come yet?' she asked. She never spoke in anything other than a normal conversational tone. No sweet talk. It annoyed me. Anything might have annoyed me then. 'Have you?' I said. 'Three times,' she said. She was smiling and smiling at me. I couldn't deal with that. 'Hang over the edge of the bed,' I said. 'I want to play with your tits.' Then I hauled her round.

After the stuff with Mora during that afternoon, I didn't think I was going to come again for a month anyway. There couldn't be anything left. So I just kept banging away at her. I wanted to see what she could do. I knew how long she'd not been a virgin and I wondered what she'd learnt. She'd learnt a lot. When I got fed up banging her over the side of the bed, I pulled her round again and set her on my cock. Even in the deficit wank situation I was in, the blowjob was brilliant. Her boyfriend obviously had her well rehearsed on that one. I was dead impressed. I had to stop her. We never mentioned her boyfriend. I put her through the menu. Everything you could do on a bed without any paraphernalia. She was a little unsure about getting fucked on her elbows and knees, but that added to the excitement. She even demonstrated how she masturbated before I gave her some head. This was good. Some of it was great, but it just went on too long. I wanted to come then, but couldn't. At the back of my mind, something was always irritating me. Maybe it was how slowly she moved. I hauled and pushed and shoved her into positions. She seemed like compliance itself. I went to sleep in a bad mood.

I thought I'd ride her first thing in the morning, but she got up and got dressed. I watched her fitting her tits into her bra. She left the room without putting on any knickers. I could hear her and Doreen talking in the corridor. I got really hard. I couldn't stop recollecting what a shameless hussy she'd been. I could have come then. I wasn't going to take a month. A night's sleep had done the trick. I was running through the scenarios and pulling my cock, but resisting orgasm. She came back into the room. I asked her to sit down for a minute. She sat down on the edge of the bed and looked down into her lap as if I was going to say something serious to her. I sprang towards her and told her I was dying to ride her. I pushed her back on to the folds of blankets and squeezed it up her without any preliminaries whatsoever. I thought of tearing off her blouse, but decided just to get it over with as quick as I could. A quick fuck. I came that time. 'You've made me all wet,' she said. 'Ah've got tae meet ma boyfriend in half an hour.' God. I rolled over and pulled the blankets back on top of me. It did not feel as if it was time yet to start the day.

I hadn't been to the boxing for a while. Everyone punched me on the nose. Wee Benny asked me if I wanted a fight. I said yes.

chapter ten

~~~~~~~~~~~~~~~

This is the last chapter. The last chapter. From the start of the school year last August till the beginning of February. With three weeks off for brain damage at Christmas and Hogmanay. Six months. Twelve hours a week. About three hundred hours. I'll be finished before my birthday.

~~~~~~~~~~~~~~~

I should really pack this in. It feels like boxing did when I packed that in. I'm not going to get any more out of this, am I? I've had a lot. About eight plays produced, a novel published, wee bits here and there. The last money I screwed out of anyone was nearly three years ago. Maybe somebody out there is trying to tell me something. Like fuck off. Robert Burns was dead about eight years ago. Jesus Christ was dead eleven years ago. I'm even older than the leader of the Labour Party. It would be nice to think that I wasn't underachieving here. I wish I could think of something else I wanted to do.

~~~~~~~~~~~~~~~

I wanted to start a magazine a year or so ago. I was still

grovelling to the BBC at the time and I thought they'd give me a few grand. If I only had a grand, I could be a millionaire! I reckon I could lose a grand easily on three issues of a magazine, especially if the parties were good. I was going to call it *The Revenge of the Bestiality Bimbos*, but I think *Legal Drugs Suck* is even better. A magazine about hypocrisy in Scottish life, written from within the establishment by potheads in suits. Maybe I should call it that. *Potheads in Suits*. Published here in Edinburgh just in time for the Scottish parliament. Second on my list after the Nullarbor once I get this megabuck book deal. Hope springs.

·····∿∿∿∿∿·····

There's sometimes a problem when you've finished a book. There's nothing left to do. A gap. At first, you might be pleased. You might be delighted. You're probably relieved. I've got a problem with this since it's not been like writing a book. Too fast. Too enjoyable. Last August I was thinking of writing something about the parallels or connections between sado-masochism and boxing, but I've forgotten what they were. If I ever knew. Maybe you can only see them if you kind of squint. It doesn't matter if you can't. I wanted to write about boxing and fornicating, and that's what I have done. If nobody wants it, too bad. I wanted it.

I've already written the first fight. I wrote that right at the beginning. I'll just have to insert it. Then I'll read it and correct some wee bits and then what will I do? I suppose I'll have to hawk it around the dyslexic bastards again. That's the worst part. That's horrible. Hopeless as well. Might as well give that a miss. I'll go back and have a look at a play I wrote last year.

~~~~~~~~~~~~~~~~~~~~~~~~~~~~~~

I wrote a play about Scotland under the fascist regime. It was set in a scrapyard which was defunct and turning into a rubbish dump and then a funeral business. There were four characters. They ended up murdering and eating bits of each other. It was a comedy. I sent it out to the four kind of directors I have sort of met and none of them wanted anything to do with it. I didn't tell them it was about Scotland under the fascist regime, so they probably thought it was about people eating each other. I wouldn't be surprised. One of them was even Scottish, no doubt with a commitment to new Scottish writing for the purposes of Arts Council, subsidies, the spending of. I haven't even sort of met him. He runs a theatre company and he never replied. Nothing fucking changes!

~~~~~~~~~~~~~~~~~~~~~~~~~~~~~~

I could become a theatre director. What a hassle! Think of how many people you could fall out with then. Hundreds of the bastards! You can be a theatre director if you want. Nobody's stopping you. The guy who put on *Busted* first of all was on eighty fags a day by the time it hit the Triangle Club in Pilton. He was going a funny colour between grey and yellow just before the show opened. On the first night of *Busted* on the Fringe the guy who was acting the main part totally blew the first scene. Couldn't get off page four. Loved page four. Went from page two to page four. Went from page six to page four at one point. For a while he just walked around, looking a bit tense. The director didn't see that bit. I heard the door slamming as he ran away.

~~~~~~~~~~~~~~~~~~~~~~~~~~~~~~

I could have a go at writing another one of these books. Make the authorial voice a bit more interesting. A murderer. A cripple. A detective. A murdering crippled detective. Write about two things you want to write about and balance them up with the intrusive authorial voice, which is me. If I managed to sell this, I'd have to write another one anyway. Then I could become a famous writer of books sort of kind of the same, but not all that much. Here's the sequel. It starts in the Nullarbor Plain. A solar-powered laptop under the big Australian sky. All about trying not to be famous when nobody wants me to be famous anyway. I'll call it *On Becoming a Housewife. Reflections on Sex and Cooking. Or, What Do You Mean You Want Some Money of Your Own?* It's a killer. A megabuck advance to me. Dream on, baby. Here comes the fight. Everybody likes a good fight. I seem to have lost this one.

We went into the main hall, into the screaming and shouting, out among the drunken red faces. Somebody in the ring was going down and getting up, and then going down again. My seconds led me to the apron of the ring, at the side where there were fewer tables facing on to the action. A man who could have come straight out of a Popeye cartoon was waiting there to glove up the fighters. He didn't have much hair, but a bent nose and a white woollen polo-necked jumper. I couldn't believe he looked like such a cliché.

Another fighter was getting gloved up when I arrived. He had on the proper boxing boots and was wearing the proper silken robe. Obviously, he wouldn't be fighting me. He was too big. Couldn't be a novice with gear like that anyway. But I was trying to ignore everything. Keep cool. Stay focused. I was starting to unravel just a wee bit. A bundle of nerves, a jangle of energy, but focusing somehow without fixing my attention on anything particular. I was glad in a way I was so short-sighted.

So I waited for the boy before me to get gloved up and then it was my turn. The bent nose reached across to a table behind him and grabbed a set of old, wrinkly brown gloves. He seemed quite deliberate and certain about everything he did, making sure my hand was forced right into the glove. There's a kind of leather bar across the palm which you have to grip.

'Grip it! Grip it!' he said. I've got small hands and tiny wrists and I never did have much of a grip. 'Clench it! Make a fist! That's right.' They were eight-ounce gloves. I'd never had on a pair of eight-ounce gloves before. We sparred with sixteen-ounce gloves. The first thing you might notice about eight-ounce gloves is that you can't hide behind them.

I spent most of the time staring over the wee man's head at the haze of little red table lights, and fag smoke, and splodgy, doughy faces. It was strange being in a big open space like that without having my glasses on. I didn't have to worry about not being able to see far. The boy would be up close enough.

Then we went up an aisle, past the tables to a corner at the back of the hall where we could wait. I was a wreck when we stopped there, a shaking, twitching mess. I had to do something, anything. Bang my head on the wall, jump up and down, run. Right at that moment, I would have beaten anyone over forty yards. I was nervous energy, needing release, grounded, earthed.

'How are ye feelin'?' said Bill.

'I'm going rattle maself tae bits if we don't get on wi' this fuckin' thing!' I gibbered at him. My eyes must have been popping. He told me to punch into his hands. He held them up. I threw some punches and missed them all.

'Naw, naw,' said Wee Benny. 'Sit doon, son. Here, sit doon.' There were fold-down seats against the back wall there and Benny pushed me into one. He told me to keep my legs stretched out. They were shaking and wobbling all over the place. Whatever any other part of me wanted to do, my legs wanted to leave. The life was jumping out of them. They were really shaking.

I was glad I couldn't see the end of the fight before mine. It was a blur of violence under a bright, far-off cone of light. Someone went down for the last time. It was easy to tell it wasn't a local boy. The yelling. The referee stopped the fight. There was the pause before the announcement. I was staring towards a seat not far away, into the back of someone's head.

'Let's get down there,' said Bill the Trainer. I jumped to my feet. 'Follow me an' Benny doon the aisle. Don't pay any attention tae whit anyone says, or shouts at ye either!'

I stared at the space between their heads as I went down the aisle. Doing was better than waiting. As I passed the tables nearer the front, which were laid out to end in parallel lines, jibes, mainly about my hair, were slung at my back. But I was above all that. I had to feel above it somehow and this feeling came very easily. The crowd suddenly meant nothing to me. Drunks. Pissheads. Wankers.

I realised my face was as flat as a pancake. It wasn't trying to talk to anyone or hold any particular expression. I had a blank face. My eyes were looking at nothing in particular, a flat, myopic stare. Most of what I'd felt at the corner up the back had dissolved into something else far more intense and concentrated. I didn't feel fragile. I felt the way I should feel. Psychokiller.

'And the next contest will be a middleweight contest . . .' I heard that part of the announcement all

143

right. I was fourteen pounds lighter than that and assumed it was a mistake.

I watched a scrum of people push behind the winner of the previous bout as he made his way round the near side of the ring. I didn't look at him. Then I was told to stand in a cat litter. 'Whit's that?' 'Resin,' Bill said. 'Stops your feet slipping.' I was up the steps first and ducked in under the ropes. Lots of light. It's very bright up there and everything else is dimmed in comparison, all the little red lights even fuzzier. It's like boxing in a dark room on the top of a snooker table. There was no one else in there with me till Bill and Benny came through the ropes. Both had started chewing gum.

'Go round the ring and get a feel of the ropes,' said Bill.

So I moved around and bounced off each set of ropes and it must have looked then as if I knew how to use the ropes, which I didn't. The boards under the canvas were very springy. I looked down at it. Speckles of blood. Then the other boxer and his two handlers got into the ring. I knew they were there and I knew the other boxer was the one who'd got gloved up before me, but I wasn't looking at them, not directly. I could hear the cheers as they climbed into the ring. I went back to bouncing off the four sets of ropes and then back to my corner. What a lot of jeering there was then. I stood in the corner, jiggering about, staring over the post.

'The ref wants to talk to you. Get out there,' said Bill and I went into the middle of the ring, still trying not to look at anything in particular.

'Now, Ah want youse both . . .' the ref started, but I didn't hear too much else. I was staring at the boy's boxing boots and my eyes started slowly coming up the length of his body. Real boxing shorts. Red vest. I wasn't accustomed to looking people in the eyes. Not right in the eyes. When

I spoke to people I looked at their chins, or noses, or something, but I knew I'd have to look this person in the eye, so I looked into his eyes right then. I stared into his eyes. He was slightly shorter. He was more thickset, but slightly shorter. And I stared into his eyes. 'Shake,' said the ref. We clasped gloves and I didn't stop staring into his eyes.

'Now, get back tae your corners an' when the bell rings, come out fightin'.

Bill slipped the gumshield in and they were talking to me, but I wasn't listening. Ah'll kill him. Ah'll kill him, Ah'll kill him, I kept saying to myself and it wasn't because I was scared, though I was. I was saying Ah'll kill him because in the terror and excitement of it all that's what I wanted to do to him. I did want to hit him as hard and as often as I could. Hearing me saying Ah'll kill him, Ah'll kill him over and over kind of scared me as well.

The great thing about boxing is that you get the A to Z. You're not stuck emotionally between P and S. You can get scared. You can get amazed. You can get totally exhilarated. Unfortunately, you can also get killed, though that is very rare. But the fact does add spice. Ah'll kill him. Ah'll kill him, Ah'll kill him resonates in all kinds of ways. Ding! Ding!

It's a long way to the centre of the ring. I'd been told the first rule in boxing is control the centre of the ring. This means you can always put your opponent under pressure, forcing him on to his back foot. He also has longer distances to cover than you and therefore has to work harder.

But it's a long way to the centre of the ring and when you get there, you've got to make the other guy not want to be there as much as you.

So he loomed towards me, growing bigger and bigger like a rock rolling downhill. And there he was right in front of me, coming into range. I locked on to his eyes. The slightest flicker and I threw out a left. Bang! Right through his guard, which opened up as he threw the first punch. Be first. Be first doesn't mean throw first, though it can mean that. I told myself to throw a straight left every time his eyes moved. Your eyes move a little when you start to throw a punch. Twitch. Bang! I hit him a second time. Straight left straight into the face. That knocked him back a little and I moved forward and he backed off. Then he threw another left which lacked conviction and he got hit again. I'd thrown three punches and hit him three times. I could have been a contender, Charlie.

He was moving back towards the ropes and his eyes were suddenly flickering, and I didn't think he was frightened. I was concentrating too hard to shape a thought like that, but something in me knew it. For just a moment, fear shook his eyes off centre and a horrible kind of cruel, rictus leer came on to my face. I thought I had him. I'd frightened him. I thought I'd won the fight. The fight must then have lasted all of seven or eight seconds.

He bounced off the ropes and suddenly he was well out of range and moving round the side. He knew how to use the ropes. And he seemed to move easier than me, going backwards faster than I could go forwards. My legs felt stiff as I moved round after him, feeling tense and selfconscious somehow. I could hear the crowd. What a noise! I knew I wasn't slipping and sliding along like I was supposed to. Then he came forwards again, and I had to hit him again, and keep him going back. I wasn't holding the centre of the ring then. I was chasing him, but I wasn't catching him.

Sometimes he moved and sometimes I moved him. And when he stopped to fight, I'd mostly move in and then move out. And then started backing him up again. He wasn't getting to fight the way he wanted to. He was moving back again and was in his own corner. Trapped in the corner. I feinted with a left and hit him with a good right. Then I did the exact same thing again.

Ding! Ding!

I hurried all the way across the ring, thinking I'd trapped the boy in his corner, only later realising he'd gone back there to wait for the bell. The stool was waiting for me with Bill and Wee Benny.

'Where did ye learn that wi' the right?' said Bill. I was gasping in huge lungfuls of air and was unable to respond. A little blood and snotters was wiped off my face with the sweat, and 'Spit into that,' he said, holding up the bucket. During all this Wee Benny was hurling advice excitedly from somewhere to the side, but Bill was right in my face.

'That was a good round. You've won it. Now, listen to me. This boy is goiny get told tae come out an' fight. Don't stand an' fight him, right? Dae ye hear me?'

'Yeah.'

'Box him, don't fight. Hit him an' move. Good boy.'

Ding! Ding!

'Off you go!'

Going out for the second felt much better than going out for the first. The awful tension was gone. We weren't shy of each other. The tentativeness had disappeared. There was no need to feel apologetic any more.

He'd got up off his stool early and was waiting for me in the middle of the ring. He beat his fists together. He seemed unafraid. He looked as if the centre of the ring was his. This is when the fight started to get a little bit brutal because when I sailed up to him I almost immediately forgot what Bill had told me. Don't fight. When I hit him this time, he didn't move back but stayed there. He was taking it and dishing it out and I wasn't moving in and out like I was supposed to. I was waiting there and we started knocking the fuck out of each other.

We boxed on. Then he was moving away again and I was following him, a little stiff-legged but getting too tired to be uptight and self-conscious. He stopped. I went towards him holding my left hand too far forward, just hanging it out there. Whack! A right hook came round it and thudded into my head just at eye level. It was one of those kind of blows where you don't see stars, and it doesn't go black then white, and you don't lose consciousness. It was the kind of blow which just stops you for two or three seconds. You don't really move. Everything goes stop and then starts again.

And when it started again, I did exactly the same thing. Whack! A bit lower and it might have been curtains. But it was just a little lower than the last one. A stunner. Stunned. Waiting. Start again. I stepped back. I moved in and moved out quickly as he was throwing another one. He missed and the force of the blow pulled him off balance so that his face was staring over at me. Bang, bang! Two lefts to the head and push him back again. Hit him again. Push him back again.

Then he was going round and round in circles and I waited in the middle of the ring. And when it seemed indecorous to keep going round, he closed with me, but you could see his heart wasn't in it. Even I could hear his corner screaming at him. Then we were standing in the middle of the ring again, knocking the fuck out of each other again.

Ding! Ding!

'That was crap!' said Bill, splashing me with the sponge

as I slumped on to the stool. 'Ah told ye no tae fight, didn't Ah? So don't fuckin' fight, right?'

Suddenly, he had the sponge at the back of my neck and beautifully cold water ran down my spine, my back almost arching as my eyes widened and I pulled in a sharp breath. Electric chill.

'Deep breaths! Deep breaths!' said Bill. Wee Benny was fanning me with a towel.

'Only one tae go. One tae go,' he repeated.

'This is a home-town boy,' said Bill, staring into my face. 'Now you've won one an' you've lost one. You've got tae win this one. But don't fight him. Hit and move! Hit and move! Remember he's tireder than you are!'

Ding! Ding!

'On ye go!'

One more to go. It didn't matter now if I got knocked down or knocked out. Nothing could humiliate me. I couldn't disgrace myself now. I'd done my best. And there he was, waiting in the middle of the ring, punching his fists together.

One of the things that attracted me to boxing was that I doubted my ability to compete. I'm really not a competitive person. When I was a young hippy student kind of a person, I told myself that I'd chosen not to compete. I could compete if I wanted to. Or could I? If you're worried about your ability to compete, try and win a boxing match. All this other stuff like running around tracks and jumping over things is just a lot of old sublimation. Boxing is competition red in tooth and claw. A testosterone hustle. When I went out for that third round, I wanted to win. I wanted to be the winner. He could stand in the middle of

the ring beating his fists together as long as he liked. Ding
ding and I'd be there with him.

~~~~~~~~~~

You move in and move back, and move in. You always
keep the other guy almost in range, and you engage when
you want to engage, not when he wants to. I couldn't
punch like him and he couldn't jab like me. But I knew
when I got hit because of the bellowing of the crowd.
When I hit him it quietened down, but it wasn't ever
quiet. It was a variation on a roar.

He was getting frustrated because I wasn't going to
fight and was winning behind the jab. He started rushing
me, but it's easier to box going back if you're slightly taller
with a decent jab. So I jabbed and moved back and he
was rushing in when I came back onto my front foot and
slam! Hard straight right bang in the middle of his face.
A slow-motion shot as the punch spread his nose to the
left, and when it came back the blood started running on
to his moustache.

A bang on the nose will impair your sight for a few
seconds as your eyes blur and water. But he'd come right
onto it and he was staggering backwards towards the
ropes. I followed him. I really wanted to hit him then. No
mercy. No quarter. He came off the ropes on to a left and
right combination and then he was holding his gloves up
and moving back towards my corner. I hit him with a left
right to the top of the head, and another left right. I didn't
understand what was happening. He'd been holding his
gloves up round his head and crouching, but then he
started to sway from side to side as if he was standing on
the deck of a pitching ship. He was not throwing punches
back. I didn't know what I'd done to him, but he was well
and truly fucked.

I noticed my hair had started to fall on to my face and stepped back to sweep it away.

'Forget your fuckin' hair!' Wee Benny was shouting. 'Hit him! Hit him!'

The boy was still going back and I caught him twice again before he reached the ropes. He was bending over and swaying there and I could hear Wee Benny screaming at me.

'Keep his chin up! Keep his chin up!'

If someone is bending and swaying on the ropes, you should throw in some uppercuts. This keeps the person's chin up so you can slam it, but I didn't know how to throw an uppercut, so I banged him again on top of the head. I couldn't understand why he wasn't fighting back. Suddenly, the bell went.

Ding! Ding!

What a wonderful sound! It was over. A mixture of joy and relief consumed me. The other boy lifted his head and his eyes met mine and he looked half drunk, half startled when I threw my arms round him. Then I threw my arms round the referee. Then I went over to the boy's corner and the seconds knew they'd lost, but they're always good.

'Fargs varima,' I said, or whatever it sounded like through the gumshield.

Then I went back into the corner and Bill and Benny were in the ring, their faces beaming with delight. They were slapping my back and wiping my face and pulling my gumshield out. I was completely delirious by then.

'A unanimous decision . . . ' The MC was holding my hand up. I clasped the boy's hand and nodded.

Poisonous, and the Assistant Head, and Doreen and Jerry were in the fourth row. Drunk and waving their arms as

I leant over the ropes. 'Did you like it?' I bawled down at
them, stretching my arms out. As high as kites, they leapt
about. None of us had ever been to a boxing show before.
What a night! Down in a miners' club in Dalkeith. It was
raining outside. Jerry and I had just been staggering
around the toilets shouting. The hippies won! The hippies
won? They were out there at the edge of the car park
somewhere, waving at a taxi. I was running across the
open space when I dropped my bag. Bending to pick it
up when this big white car suddenly comes screaming
towards me.

That's called melodrama. Like what you get in the movies.
The thing with Mora and me just stopped because there
was no point in it any more. No hard feelings. No bad
words. We could have finished on a handshake, but
nobody had to say anything. Maybe sometime in your life
you just need a friend to hold your hand and walk with you
along some ill-lit streets.

About twelve years ago, I had a video player in my flat
for the first time. I had a week off. I was on my own. I
had a gramme of speed. I went along to the video shop
and got out the Martin Scorsese movies I hadn't seen.
Also what I assumed would be a tits and bum video. My
first dirty video. Could hardly believe my eyes. About a
brothel for women. This woman at the end had sex with
twenty-four men. The shop closed down. I was told the
big chain video shops don't stock that kind of video. It'll
be on satellite though, eh? I wonder if it's harmful? All
that riding and fucking and shagging in people's living

rooms. Probably. Bound to do somebody's head in somewhere, sometime. Might lead to violence against women.
Get these horny geeks along to boxing gyms. How's that
for a bit of sublimation?

Some time after me and Mora had stopped shagging and
fucking and riding each other, I told the Assistant Head
about it when I was drunk. And he told Poisonous. And
Poisonous told Jerry. Jerry could have been a lot more
pissed off than he was. We'd moved on by then. After
an argument with our landlord about who was going to
Australia and who fucking wasn't, Jerry gave me a loan of
his velvet jacket and a nice pair of trousers. He also put
on a velvet jacket and a nice pair of trousers. The new
landlord said he'd just finished renting to a couple of
students. Fucking students. What a shame for him! We
got evicted again after four or five months. I could write
a book about that.